LOST IN NORTH AMERICA

LOST IN NORTH AMERICA

The Imaginary Canadian
in
The American Dream

JOHN GRAY

Talonbooks　　　Vancouver　　　1994

Published with the assistance of the Canada Council.

Talonbooks
201 - 1019 East Cordova
Vancouver, British Columbia
Canada V6A 1M8

Typeset in Garamond and printed and bound in Canada by Hignell Printing Ltd..

First Printing: August 1994

Canadian Cataloguing in Publication Data

Gray, John, 1946-
    Lost in North America

    ISBN 0-88922-350-5

    1. Canada—Humor. 2. National characteristics, Canadian—Humor. I. Title.
PS8563.R422L67 1994   C814'.54C94-910662-3
PR9199.3.G72L67 1994

To my fearless mother

CONTENTS

INTRODUCTION

*Every age and every nation has certain characteristic
vices, which prevail almost universally, which scarcely
any person scruples to avow, and which even rigid moral-
ists but faintly censure. Succeeding generations change
the fashion of their morals, with the fashion of their hats
and their coaches; take some other kind of wickedness
under their patronage, and wonder at the depravity of
their ancestors.*

—Lord Macaulay

Here in British Columbia, we have become used to early morning
telephone calls from back east, where people frequently forget
about the existence of time zones. I suppose they in turn complain
that we wake them up in the middle of the night.

The pleasant female voice belonged to the Clerk of the
Standing Committee on Citizenship and Immigration, conducting a
review of the Canada Citizenship Act: Would I appear before the
Committee to share my thoughts on the matter?

I had heard about these federal activities. *The Globe and Mail*
had run a story about invitations to celebrities with a conspicuously
Canadian identification—Peter Gzowski, Margaret Atwood,
Stompin' Tom Conners, we all know the list—to talk about the
meaning of Canada. Later, a CBC radio news report—in a
Discouraging Canadiana sidelight delivered with masochistic rel-
ish—indicated that few of these emblematic figures were interested
in doing so. Some had declined out of a reluctance to "become
involved politically"; others simply could not be bothered. A few
were honest enough with themselves to admit that they knew
nothing about the matter.

More honest, I'm afraid, than I.

Clearly, my name had been drawn from the bottom of the
barrel.

Of course I had been through this sort of thing before, many
times. During the Progressive Conservative reign, their urbane
Minister of Communications hosted periodic think tanks in which
culture-types sat around tables in rented conference rooms and

complained about Canada. Marcel Masse, a Quebecer, seemed perplexed and amused by everything he saw and heard in English Canada, and could launch into the most impressive extemporaneous rants you ever heard—about the need to decolonize both Quebec *and* Canada, how his ministry established the context for all other ministries, how difficult life was for a sensitive human being in the current economic climate. He was always elegantly turned out, yet his skin exhibited a slightly uneasy glow, as though he wished someone would open a window.

The Minister, as he put it, needed our "'elp." Our minds were to provide him with ammunition, with which to repel the forces of philistinism approaching from a westerly direction. He was our champion, out to slay the dragon of ignorance on our behalf—or so the argument went. Culture ministers use it all the time to gather a constituency for their issues and to insulate themselves from personal abuse.

We would gather in the upper room of an upscale hotel. The Minister would gaze about the table thoughtfully with large, liquid eyes, like a benevolent patriarch, as we intense men and women in leather and denim poured out our hearts over coffee and muffins, surrounded by bureaucrats with blank faces and Mont Blanc pens, scribbling like mad.

We would talk about all sorts of things: how to improve the "status of the artist"; whether the "cultural industries" would be better served under the umbrella of the Environment Ministry or the Defence Ministry; how to make the artist less dependent on government—that sort of thing. We could go on for hours; and if you keep doing anything long enough, you can convince yourself that you are really getting somewhere.

Later we would all enjoy a last supper together and go home, and never hear another word about it.

But despite a profound sense of futility, of being the butt of a long-term practical joke, I never failed to attend these events. It was something you just *did*—like jury duty. Serving on panels is a cultural form of conscription—painful, inconvenient and boring, yet deeply thrilling at the same time, for you feel yourself to be contributing in an unspecified way to something greater than yourself.

Now the Committee on Citizenship and Immigration was calling me to action. I thought I knew even less about immigration than I knew about culture, but this did not deter me, for it is widely accepted that the Canadian government knows more about what goes on in the minds of Canadians than we know ourselves. My task was not to wonder why; again I had been called upon to serve the Parentland, and again I would not refuse. Ready, aye, ready.

Unlike M. Masse however, the Clerk of the Committee gave me a choice of two appearance modes: I could fly to Ottawa, all expenses paid, to appear before the Committee—which seemed extravagant for the meagre insight I had to offer—or I could take advantage of state-of-the-art electronics and appear via something called a "teleconference."

Without knowing precisely what it was, a teleconference seemed ideal—sleek and contemporary, reeking of virtual reality and the Global Village. I imagined it to be like reading the news on TV, or doing a double-end interview on *Midday*. For some reason, images of *Star Trek* came to mind. As things turned out, it wasn't at all like that. In hindsight, it would have been less mortifying had I flown to Ottawa.

The voice of the Clerk assigned me a date and time for my teleconference, together with a Vancouver address. A day later, somebody called back to say that the address had been changed. Then the time was corrected—my appointment had in error been scheduled for *Ottawa* time. Had I arrived at the appointed hour, I should have been three hours late and everyone would have gone home.

Next day, an eighteen-page fax snaked its way onto my kitchen floor, bearing the House of Commons letterhead with its heraldic coat-of-arms and the hopeful legend, *Ad Mari usque ad Mare*. The covering letter was so respectful, my chest swelled with pride:

> *The members of the Committee feel strongly that it is Canada's writers and artists who best express the spirit and meaning of citizenship....*

Only when I tried to compose something to say to the Committee, something that would "express the spirit and meaning of citizenship," did I ask myself exactly what that sentence meant, and whether its implied assumptions were indeed true.

Immediately, I was in trouble.

Precisely in what way do Canada's writers and artists *do* that? Stompin' Tom Connors may be as Canadian as Insulbrick, but when he wrote "Bud the Spud," did he mean to say that driving a produce truck from PEI to Ontario had something to do with *citizenship?*

I tried to imagine a new immigrant from, say, Sri Lanka, parsing the lyrics to "Sudbury Saturday Night," searching for the meaning of Canadian citizenship:

Oh Momma's playin' bingo
And Daddy's gettin' stinko
'Cause there's no one down at INCO
On a Sudbury Saturday night...

Even a sampling of more highfalutin' Canadian culture (and there is plenty of that on hand) was of no help. I thought of Atwood's existential feminist awakenings in the face of some death symbol or other; of Alec Colville's chilly artifacts depicting "normal" life, frozen into abnormality and menaced by some compositionally-induced threat. For that matter, what did the Group of Seven, with their trees and lakes and sky, have to do with *citizenship?* The more I thought on the subject, the more inadequate I felt. Feverishly I pored through the remaining seventeen waxy fax sheets for some insight as to what was required.

Entitled, elliptically, *A Citizenship Strategy,* the document did not ease my mind for, as far as I could tell, the Committee had set itself an agenda of weighty matters indeed:

1. *HOW THE VALUE AND VISIBILITY OF CANADIAN CITIZENSHIP MIGHT BE ENHANCED.*
2. *HOW THE FAIRNESS AND INTEGRITY OF CANADIAN CITIZENSHIP MIGHT BE STRENGTHENED.*

Value. Visibility. Fairness. Integrity. What did these words *mean?* How were these ideals to be attained in *any* sphere of human life, private or public? Most appalling of all, what the Hell did they mean by the word *Citizenship?* Did they intend it to describe a person, a legal status, or an action?

A person: The nineteenth-century European concept of the nation-state assumed that humanity naturally divides into "peoples" and that, in a perfect world, "a people" should have "a country" of their own to reflect their peculiar, genetically-determined beliefs and needs. However, this eugenically-based nationalist vision fell seriously out of favour with the rise of National Socialism and the war that followed. (Germany evidently felt that, as "a people," they required *more.*)

Besides, when you consider the shifting twentieth-century demographics in countries such as Canada, where every child is born equipped with officially-sanctioned hyphens to indicate multiple cultural affiliations, this vision of citizenship seems rather tricky to apply.

A legal status: More likely, "citizenship" is meant to signify some sort of legal covenant—especially given the preponderance of lawyers in government. But if it refers to a legal contract, then it is an extremely one-sided one. To begin with, citizenship is awarded upon birth: The state grants the citizen with *a priori* rights, whereas the citizen, having been proclaimed so *in utero,* has not admitted to any responsibilities in return. If Canadian citizenship is a legal contract, then it has been signed by only one party. The citizen can hold the nation to its end of the bargain, yet remain free to break or abrogate the contract at will—or even to sign a contract with another nation at the same time. Some contract.

An action: Or perhaps "citizenship" refers to a number of responsibilities the citizen agrees to undertake: to vote, for example, or to pay one's taxes, or to give one's opinion to government hearings when asked. But how then can such a citizenship indicate a *permanent* status? How does it apply, say, to the expatriate retiree who plans to die in Florida, or to the dual citizen born outside the country who has never set foot in Canada? With what actions are they meant to express their citizenship on an ongoing basis?

I do not know any two Canadians who will agree on these things, and for that reason we hate to talk about it at all. We never discuss what citizenship means in school, nor do we debate it in our national media: how then are we to explain it to the recently-arrived dentist from Uganda, or to the Jamaican restauranteur?

The covering letter went on to explain that I would have ten minutes in which to share my thoughts on these issues, after which I might be asked some questions by members of the Committee. Ten minutes to discuss the meaning, value, and integrity of

Canadian citizenship: Clearly I had been called upon to write a *haiku*.

For two days I worked on my statement. I pictured myself facing a recent immigrant, clutching my pithy statement about Canadian citizenship, my one precious kernel of meaning to guide him or her in their new life. But this miracle of minimalist eloquence eluded me, and in my imagination I stammered, perspired, and babbled on.

I implored the Kenyan bank teller not to believe what she sees on television and in movies, newspapers and magazines. I cautioned her that these media images and slogans do not represent Canada; that despite the evidence of our cultural media, Canadians are not a confrontational people—on the contrary, our guiding public principle is a spirit of accommodation, a mutual granting of peripheral space expressed and embodied by the landscape itself, enabling Canadians, however hyphenated, to get along.

I explained to the Italian pharmacist that this ethic of accommodation is continually at risk, thanks to cultural and geographical distance and the domination of our media by more monolithic and confrontational cultures; that to find Canada, one must turn off the TV and the radio, and watch how people behave in their own town, on their own street.

Canadians resent littering, but will not complain if you do. They can be belligerent, but will apologize when they bump into you—sometimes even when you bump into *them*. You are unlikely to be shouted at, hit, or shot by a Canadian, unless he has been drinking or there has been a terrible mistake. If you look about in real life, again and again you will find evidence of an implicit accord that is the basis of the Canadian way of life, and it is up to Canadians to maintain it for our own sake and for our children....

Thus I babbled. Even now, reading this, I fight the urge to erase the document. Though appropriate to a Dominion Day luncheon speech, as food for the Standing Committee it seemed like thin gruel indeed.

At the appointed hour I entered a shoebox-like building and climbed the stairs to a floor stocked with rented office equipment, belonging to a company that deals in audio-visual technology. The office was temporary and entirely without character—a couple of workmen could gut it to the wall studs in a matter of hours.

The dark-skinned receptionist gave me a lovely, telegenic smile and invited me to sit down. Five minutes later, a tall woman in a pink suit shook my hand, then ushered me down a hall and into an empty boardroom, where she indicated a seat at the end of a long table.

I sat. Before me on the table crouched a gadget about the size of a speaker phone. At the other end of the table loomed a giant video projection screen, on which a group of people talked soundlessly around another table—the kind of stock shot you see on Parliamentary television. Some wore translation devices in their ears. Behind them, assistants bustled back and forth, gathering and distributing memos. The large screen and the bright, flat lighting rendered the picture fuzzy and pastel. If this was virtual reality, then it was far more virtual than real.

I looked uneasily at the woman in the pink suit: "Do I need to clip on a mike or something?"

"No, no. They can hear you." She smiled down at me as she exited, closing the door behind her. I was alone—or perhaps not.

"Mr. Gray?" An unfamiliar female voice rattled over the tiny speaker. "Are you with us?"

"Yes," I replied, without knowing who she was or what she meant by "with us." Then, almost immediately, I heard *my own voice* through the speaker: "Yes," the voice said, nervously.

"Hello, Mr. Gray," she repeated.

"How do you do," I replied.

"How do you do?" echoed the little speaker, in a thin parody of my own voice.

My heart sank, for I knew what was up. Most of us have been a party to one of those transatlantic satellite calls in which you hear your own voice echo back at half-second intervals. This electronic quirk distorts the rhythm of conversation entirely, forcing the speaker to choose between utter cacophony and the stilted communication of robots. It becomes impossible to talk, hear or think.

Then to my horror I saw someone on screen, situated in a panel near the lower right-hand corner, like the sign language interpreter on cable television.

My God, it was me.

Evidently that gadget on the conference table contained both a mike and a hidden camera, for there I was on screen, fuzzy and pastel, staring back at myself. In a visual counterpart to the echo effect, I could watch my every move mirrored before me—after a split second's delay. No, it was worse: I was not mirrored, but *photographed*. I could see myself *as others saw me*.

As any actor knows, to perform and observe yourself perform at the same time is the surest way to achieve disaster on stage. The mind simply will not work that way. It is like trying to drive, looking through the windshield and the rear-view mirror at the same time.

The disembodied female voice invited me to begin my presentation, reminding me with gentle firmness that I was limited to ten minutes—"so that there will be lots of time for questions." Her accent sounded Ontarian, her tone Presbyterian. I envisaged a tailored suit or sweater set, pearls, stylish eyeglasses and a large watch.

I began. I delivered my pathetic homilies about accommodation and decency and, as predicted, the voice that stammered back at me—my own voice—rattled me. Though I knew it was a mistake, irresistibly I glanced up at myself. My movements appeared false and uncoordinated—I seemed rather Nixonesque. I had never seen myself as Richard Nixon before. I tried to adjust my expression to something more telegenic, made myself look worse, and lost my train of thought. I dug my wretched, glowering mug back into my manuscript and concluded.

There followed a long pause, then: "Are you finished?"

The voice sounded slightly incredulous—*Is that all?* Then for no reason that I could see, a man with thin reddish hair and spectacles appeared on the screen, turned to the person beside him, and laughed soundlessly, in stop-motion: no doubt enjoying a joke at the expense of the idiot from Vancouver.

I looked away, sheepishly, as did my screen persona. "Yes," I replied, miserably. "That's about it."

"I see. Well, perhaps there are some questions."

Another man appeared—balding, wearing an ear piece and speaking in French. Almost immediately, the voice of a translator crackled through the tiny speaker. Now I could hear a man speaking in French, a translator speaking in English, and could see and hear my own reactions a split second after they occurred. I tried to keep track of everything, perspiring freely.

The gentleman, clearly with the Bloc Québécois, wanted to know how I felt about the two "founding nations."

16

I paused. The screen waited, silently. All of Ottawa stood on hold as expensive satellite moments ticked by.

"Mr. Gray? Are you there?"

My mind darted about like a trapped squirrel. What did he mean by "founding nations"? Was he referring to France and England—European nation-states that fought over this and other colonial territories during the Hundred Years War? Surely not: that would be an intolerably colonial assumption for a party aspiring to sovereignty for Quebec. Or did "founding nations" refer to Quebec and "the Rest of Canada," as though the split had already occurred? But if so, how were those two nations represented in our governments—at a time when both the Government of Canada and the Official Opposition were led by *Quebecers?* Had Quebec separated from *itself?*

Or was this all just a translation problem? Did the word *nation* have a slightly different meaning in French than in English? Perhaps *nation*, in French, refers to "a people," in the same way that native people refer to the "Cree nation"—which clearly does not imply the kind of European nation-state the English word does.

My face stared back at me on screen with a poleaxed expression: I had no idea what he meant by the word "nation." What was I to say?

Echoed on screen and over the little speaker, I saw and heard myself chatter on about the nation-state as a European colonial artifact, that to talk about "founding nations" arbitrarily cut off the land from thousands of years of its history and allowed extinct versions of England and France—nation-states now in the process of surrendering part of their "sovereignty" to the European Common Market—to continue to hold Canada in their rigor mortis grip....

My televised audience fidgeted soundlessly in stop-action. I imagined hundreds of eyes rolling toward the ceiling, in unison. In my mind I begged myself to stop talking, and eventually my mouth conceded.

Another middle-aged gentleman appeared on screen, wearing a sports jacket and aviator spectacles—perhaps he was with the Reform Party. "Mr. Gray," he queried, "what *is* a Canadian? Can you give me a definition of a Canadian?"

I fought a sudden urge to get up and bolt from the room. Here was one Canadian asking another Canadian to tell him to define a Canadian—like the clarinet player turning to the trumpet player and asking where the band is. And on television, to boot. What was he asking for? Did he want me to describe *him?* Did he want me to describe *me?* Or did he want me to describe somebody else?

Undeterred by my mind's incomprehension, my mouth began to move. I rambled on about villages and settling patterns, about the myth of the north, survival and the cold; I even heard myself talking about the *weather,* while the voice in my brain shrieked, *Stop this! You are babbling!* Yet my mouth refused to stop. There was no rhythmic end to the speech, no natural place to conclude that made any kind of a point.

Then they asked me what I thought about the Queen. And what did I think of multiculturalism?

It was like digging for the Oak Island treasure: Every time we reached what seemed to be the bottom, we broke through to another layer of muck. Perhaps the hole went clear through to China.

Mercifully, they soon tired of me. The voice thanked me for my "insights" and, as though at a signal, the woman in the pink suit ushered me and my insights out the door, shook my hand, and I was released.

I left the building with the self-loathing of someone who has allowed himself to become embroiled in one of those Meaning of Life discussions against his better judgement. My mind felt as though it had been covered in batter and French fried.

Whose reality was reflected by the Standing Committee on Citizenship and Immigration? Whose interests were served? Was this part of some kind of mystical rite, like the Spicer Commission—an encounter group for Canadians to get things off the national chest? Or was it like that peculiar incident a couple of months before the Conservative defeat, when the Prime Minister assembled his cabinet at the grave of Sir John A. MacDonald and awaited inspiration in a seance-like atmosphere?

We seem to be having a wee bit of trouble communicating up here, somewhere in North America. Canadians have no idea what to believe and what not to believe, while current trends—from the "information highway" to the "global economy"—simultaneously jam us together and tear us apart. One thing we do know: It doesn't feel good.

This eerie, surrealistic feeling of being caught in a dream and unable to wake up is the inspiration for this book.

Recently I have come to understand what a deeply conservative person I am, for I believe that there is such a thing as reality—that real life exists, even if you are in a dream; that, when you act on the basis of a dream, sooner or later that false belief will collide with the way things really are, and the dream will collapse like a house of cards; that, if you base your actions on dreams, there is a chance you will wake up *in* that house of cards, tumbling down on top of you.

If there is such a thing as real life, understanding it is a matter of personal survival.

Increasingly, I sense a dream-like quality to life in Canada, at the close of the twentieth century. Our national vice is our addiction to the culture of avoidance. We are the villagers in *The Emperor's New Clothes*, unwilling to admit to what is there before our eyes; perhaps we cannot allow ourselves to see the nakedness of the forces that have made us what we are.

I want to know what this dream consists of—where it begins and ends. Then, before I die, I want a glimpse—just a peek would be fine—of real life; of how things work and how they don't; of what we have in common and what we don't; of who and where we really are, and who and where we are not.

Lost in North America is an attempt to obtain a glimpse, a snapshot, of the collective imagination at work in Canada—without babbling the way I babbled to the Standing Committee on Citizenship and Immigration. Of course it is subjective—how could it not be? It would take, in Brian Mulroney's unforgettable phrase, "an unbecoming degree of temerity" for me to presume that my version of reality applies to you.

As a middle-aged, English-speaking, bicycle-riding, male-parent of Scots-Protestant descent, I define myself according to a shifting grid of hyphens, limited further by my damaged set of ears, eyes and antennae.

In that sense, this series of essays is a message in a bottle, thrown into the sea; a gesture of faith, by my publisher no less than myself, that we still have something in common.

I am grateful to Karl and Christy Siegler for their pragmatic optimism in this regard, and to my family, Beverlee, Zach and Ezra, who can accept this preoccupied man who disappears for days like an opossum in his cranial burrow, then welcome him home upon his return.

DEATH BY METAPHOR:
IT'S NOT WHAT YOU SAY, BUT HOW YOU SAY IT

In the Beginning Was the Word

Think of words as little institutions—miniature software corporations with their own structure and function. Like their macro counterparts, some words have more content than others. Some words mean nothing at all. Some words can, like certain Alberta trust companies, betray the very people who trust them the most.

Both word and institution are vulnerable to structural petrification and inner decay, in which meaning and purpose disappear, to be replaced by a dominant emotion—usually fear. Meaninglessness and chaos are the same thing, and chaos scares the spit out of us.

As meaning drains away, both the word and the institution drift into dreamland, an imaginary place that has at best a nodding acquaintance with the real life from which it sprang. Still, as Jacob and Carl Jung and Lady Macbeth discovered, dreams affect real life profoundly in many ways.

"General Motors" has become, not just a car maker, but a mental receptacle for Americans' anxiety over their loss of competitive edge and creative vigour. Likewise, "Unemployment Insurance" has become, not just an insurance plan, but a container for our fear that we have lost our compassion, our sense of fairness, our progressive optimism. Though riddled with faults, both institutional structures endure in their present form, not because they produce good cars or good service, but because of the fear associated with their demise.

In the same way, seemingly ordinary words like *victim, community, politician, crime, technology, family* and *job* have become symbolic vessels whose emotional contents have all but replaced their original function in the language.

The more these words proliferate, the more difficult it becomes for us to make sense to one another.

For a car manufacturer, the triumph of shape over substance eventually shows up in safety recalls, discontinued models, layoffs, and padlocked gates. The entropic effects of a decaying language on the imaginary life of a nation, though more subtle, can be in their own way just as disastrous.

California Dreaming

According to a *Harper's Magazine* survey, Caucasian-Americans generally think there are from two to four times as many African-Americans in the USA than is the case.

Basic misconceptions such as this inspire an unpleasant sensation in the pit of the stomach. Many North Americans experienced a similar feeling during the Gulf War, as Iraq was magically transformed into a superpower poised to conquer the free world, and Saddam Hussein, the former US ally and weapons customer, became the Beast slouching to Bethlehem. Something weird was happening. Someone was poking at our brains.

Like the television version of the Gulf War, the survey of American opinions on racial statistics is ripe for conspiracy theories, but it may not be as sinister as that. Perhaps it is a natural product of American pop culture, with its emphasis on racially-torn cities like New York, Washington and Los Angeles. Media trend-setters tend to inhabit such cites, own valuable possessions and real estate, and become concerned when they see something upsetting through the car window on their way to work.

Or the distortion may spring from well-meant affirmative action initiatives in the film and television industry. After a week of watching police dramas one would think that a third of every force in the land was Afro-American, that black-white partnerships in squad cars were commonplace. Racial integration, as a liberal dream and a conservative nightmare, may have become a collective mental "fact."

Liberal visions often go awry that way. The final scene of the 1968 movie *Easy Rider* presents a piece of liberal propaganda in which Dennis Hopper and Peter Fonda are murdered with a shotgun from a pickup truck. Despite, or because of the obvious message, the scene inspired a number of copycat shootings—evidently, some people with pickup trucks and shotguns thought the film had had a happy ending.

Or perhaps mass confusion is the inevitable product of a TV-inspired culture that does not even try to distinguish between truth and fiction. Current affairs programs emulate suspense films for the sake of "drama" and "pace," while fictional cop shows imitate the coarseness of ENG news reports, for "realism." Newspapers like *USA Today* adopt the look of cartoons, with eye-catching colours and simple, defining captions. Still more deceptive are the bottom-feeder supermarket tabloids, which simply make things up wholesale and present them as fact.

To consumers of American culture whose mental images create the imaginary nation, the effect of this surrealistic collage is a synthetic dream-world, a collective impression driven as much by fiction as by fact, yet not recognized as such, and steaming with emotion. If the real number of African-Americans is out of proportion to the level of dread experienced by Caucasians when they hear the word *black*, the imagination simply revises the number upward to match the emotion, and the mind then accepts it as fact.

In America, something has happened to the word *black*.

The Welfare Trap

Rooting about for a Canadian counterpart to this American statistical anomaly, I settled on the word *welfare*. At parties and other gatherings of relatively informed acquaintances—college graduates mostly, current affairs addicts with paid-up subscriptions to news-magazines and newspapers—I asked the question: "How many people do you estimate are on welfare?"

The reply was as many as four times the Statistics Canada figure.

This suggests to me that, like the word *black* in America,

welfare is a word that has come to denote to Canadians, not a social program, but a fear.

Regardless of one's ideology, the word *welfare* is seen as a necessary evil. To the social democrat, welfare is a regrettable degradation inflicted on "victimized" people, erecting a wall around a chronically dehumanized underclass. To the conservative populist, welfare is a low-level swindle practised by whiners and loafers on hardworking taxpayers. Both sides agree on one thing: Welfare is a Bad Thing.

There was a time when social assistance was conceived of as an expression of Canadian generosity and compassion, all very Tommy Douglas and a Good Thing indeed, contributing to our self-respect as champions of social progress and an example to others. Canada, so the argument went, was a country in the process of becoming more civilized, where the law of the jungle was to be superseded by the law of the land.

However, in the late twentieth century, the Darwinian jungle has returned with a vengeance in new multinational colours. The world has become a global sports arena in which the social safety net has made Canada soft and uncompetitive—easy pickings for lean, disciplined economies with a yen to win. In the New World Order, social assistance is not a blessing but a fattening habit. *Welfare* no longer means assistance to people in need; rather, it has come to evoke our loss of confidence in ourselves, our lack of muscle tone, our fear.

To a materialistic society, poverty is chaos and, to a "civilized" sensibility, chaos is Hell. Whether envisaged as a disease by the right, an injustice by the left or as an embarrassment by the centre, the word *welfare* evokes primitive survival fears in an imagined country heading for chaos, in which dream logic prevails: "I don't deserve to be poor, nobody like me should be poor, therefore poor people are different from me." Or, "I'm afraid to be poor, poor people are poor, therefore I am afraid of poor people."

In the imaginary country, poor people form a separate society from the rest of us—a conscious group who identify with their status as "poor people." They communicate with one another and they make plans. They feel envious and bitter, resent their poverty, seek to do harm to people with a higher standard of living, and to undermine a society in which they have failed to succeed.

In real life, I have never met a poor person who felt this way.

Many are single mothers with no time for conspiracy; others, mentally and physically challenged in a variety of ways, need all the energy they can muster just to face the day. Poor people who do become politically active are as apt to join the Reform Party as the NDP.

Inhabiting an imaginary country, with the poor "out there" someplace like a mobilizing enemy army, Canadians then go on to debate social programs—with an intensity far out of proportion to the actual topic. Like the Caucasian estimate of the black population, our need to inflate the scale and urgency of the welfare problem to a size proportionate to our fear of poverty has distorted the meaning of the word *welfare*, to the point where we are now debating a completely different topic.

Is it any wonder our social assistance programs are in a mess? *Are* they in a mess? How do we tell?

Negative emotions contained in the word *welfare* intensify when it is juxtaposed with other empty words evoking the fear of poverty—such as *deficit*, and *unemployment*.

The word *deficit* is itself sufficient to bring on nightmares of the Great Depression and the Weimar Republic, with a sound track of Scots Protestant platitudes about Living Within Our Means—whatever that means. Powerful symbols on their own, put *deficit*, *unemployment* and *welfare* together and you have a Molotov cocktail of an image, to be ignited in the interest of whatever point you wish to score, whether a denunciation of the bureaucracy, a hymn to the dignity and importance of honest toil, a call to more restrictive immigration policies, or a cautionary parable in which the Royal Bank forecloses on the mortgage and we all have to pack our things and move out of Canada.

Whatever its ideological preoccupation, no imaginable Canadian political party is going to put the word *welfare* in a positive light. In the imaginary country, *welfare* is either a social "luxury" that will be the first to go if we fail to "live within our means," or the cruel trap of an unjust society that creates and perpetuates an underclass.

The word *welfare* will not, in our time, regain its original meaning, as a civilized, optimistic, heroic gesture of collective human kindness toward the poor: knowing that there will *always* be poor people; knowing that it may not be their fault; knowing that justice, as we desire it, does not exist in the real world.

This original meaning of *welfare* is simply no longer possible.

The idea may have been pure United Church Canadiana, but as a current political and social issue you might as well speak out in favour of bigamy.

Of course, Americans have a problem with *welfare* too: In a recent *Time*-CNN survey, only 23% of respondents agreed that the government spends too much money on "assistance to the poor," while 53% agreed that the government spends too much money on *welfare*.

The Wrath of the Canadian Victim

A similar journey into dreamland is launched in any current political debate by posing the question: "What are we to do about *crime?*"

It is safe to say that no politician seeking public office is unaware that, beyond specific urban groups, we are not experiencing a crime wave—in fact, the incidence of many crimes steadily decreases as the population ages. (Arthritis may be the greatest crime deterrent of all.)

But this must never be allowed to intrude on the heated platitudes, as politicians vow sanctimoniously to stand for "the rights of the victim" and to "get tough on crime." To discuss rehabilitation, prison conditions, antiquated laws, arbitrary sentences, overcrowded courts, despair among working-class youth, or any other topic relevant to real life crime, is to be "soft on crime," tantamount to an endorsement of crime itself.

During the last federal election, whenever the subject of crime was introduced, there ensued an unseemly scramble to link the word with other emotionally combustible symbolic words—*Poverty* in the case of the NDP, *Jobs* for the Liberals, *Victim* in the speeches of the Conservatives and Reformers, while the Bloc Québécois developed a sudden, mysterious linguistic deficiency on the topic.

Victim is an especially good button to press. Who in the world is not a "victim" of something—whether a crime, the recession, a disease, an unhappy childhood, or simply of age and injustice? As individual emotions pour into the vacuum left by the word's absent meaning, dream logic takes over and we swoon to a medley of surrealist imagery.

There are criminals and there are victims; at the scene of a crime, it is physically impossible to be both at the same time. Fine, but attempt to translate this self-evident fact from the specific to the abstract, and the newly-imagined world changes radically. Criminals and victims become, not participants in a specific incident, but two imaginary races of people, separate nations in a state of civil war.

Like Britain under attack by the Luftwaffe, victims become innocents under siege by an outside, evil force acting consciously and with a plan.

In the imaginary land of law and order, a victim cannot possibly be a criminal at the same time—that would be a contradiction in terms. Yet in the real world, this is not the case at all. A woman who murders an abusive husband is both a victim and a criminal; so is the husband, if he was beaten senseless as a child by his father while his mother cowered in a corner. In the case of family violence, the issue may not be well served by placing the victim and the criminal in eternally warring camps.

Like a Strindberg play, the mental scenarios brought on by symbolic language take on the power of dreams. Connected by their own unique logic, emotion-charged vignettes are constructed by *potential* victims to express their own terror. Thus, the debate around the word *crime* is not about crime at all, but about fear, bad dreams and preemptive rage.

Of course it is possible to imagine such a nightmare in real life, an unprecedented crime wave in which nothing short of the War Measures Act will stave off chaos—which may be precisely what is happening in the imaginary country. Our news media have an unlimited supply of crime, picking and choosing among the world's daily crop of atrocities for choice morsels and serving them up one at a time. And in the imagination, everything is equidistant: Our dreams make no distinction between here and there, between an atrocity in Uganda and a murder in Sudbury. We are far more conscious of the captured serial killer in Chicago than of the amateur gardener who lives down the street.

At a time when much of our context for world events emanates from the United States, a diminishing array of cultural tools equips us to determine what is true of Canada in the real world, and what are the mental creations of our imaginary country. We are tempted to think that, should we fail to witness these telegenic horrors in our neighbourhood, it is not because we live in a different culture but because we lag behind others on the downward spiral. The American nightmare may not yet be visible on our street, but it will be any day now.

As a random selection of thrills and chills, the media's daily supply of international crime becomes the tip of an imagined iceberg of indeterminate proportions. The sheer relentlessness of crime as a motif is interpreted by the imagination as proof of an accelerating emergency—not of a lack of creativity and a shortage of professional ethics among broadcasters, producers and writers.

Caught in a maze of symbol and myth, Canadians can hardly be blamed if we start multiplying when we should be adding. Before we know it we are afraid to go out at night onto streets that have not seen a violent crime since 1952. How ironic that we lock ourselves in our homes, when most violent crimes are committed right there—in the bedroom or the kitchen, after too many drinks, with the TV set on.

Adam and Eve

Meanwhile, in the real world, terrible things really do happen to real people.

While we slug it out over "victims," "criminals" and "abusers," there is a looming crisis between men and women, arising from unacknowledged habits and assumptions that go way, way back.

What are we to do about the misogynist aspect of our cultural heritage—that ancient theme intrinsic to the Bible, the Koran, the Pentateuch, and supported by billions of men and women all over the world? Can men and women ever treat each other as civilized equals, with the narratives of Genesis and Guinevere and the *Arabian Nights* swimming around our heads?

During the 1960s, when the virgin monogamous union—a Medieval poetic conceit never intended for home use—became an acknowledged anachronism thanks to *The Kinsey Report* and the Pill, how did that affect men who were brought up with the romantic ideal branded on their spinal cords?

As recently as the 1960s, most Canadian men assumed that they would marry a virgin, that only death would part them, that a "broken home" was an inherently bad thing, and that a working wife meant that hubby had failed. If a woman "slept around" before marriage, she was "cheap." A young man, on the other hand, was expected to go through a bachelor period of "feeling his oats" with a series of "cheap" women, before he "fell in love."

With a man's true love, only the highest standards of sexual conduct applied; on the other hand, in the case of transitional, "cheap" women, "no" did not necessarily mean no, but represented a coy symbolic gesture in a traditional dance of resistance and conquest, to spice the contemporary mating ritual, late at night, in the back seat of Dad's Buick Roadmaster.

Catch You with Another Man, That's the End

Dominance based on an implied physical threat, on a chest-thumping willingness to fight to the death, was and still is the inbred ethic of thousands of Canadian males. In the imaginary country, violence is the measure of conviction, and death is the great leveller. How many Canadian men will come out and say that it is wrong to kill or die for what you believe?

In the current era of feminist awareness, what level of the male psyche endures in a more savage place, and would rather fight than switch? Given that many men have not changed, why are women attracted to them anyway? In what ways do women act as accomplices in our failure to civilize the relationship?

Naturally, in Canada we do not talk about any of this stuff. These days, violence happens, not between men and women, but between "victims" and "abusers." As vicarious victims, the public seeks a justice system that will express her justified rage, revile the abuser, and speak out against "violence against women."

All quite irrelevant, but it sets the mind at rest.

In an article about "date rape" in the campus newspaper at the University of New Brunswick, some ill-advised math professor articulated a set of sexual beliefs common to virtually every pre-1960s Canadian male, and to contemporary Christian, Moslem and Jewish traditionalists as well: that the "sexually experienced" woman operates under a different set of rules than the virgin.

According to this world view, horny young men are natural hazards, wild stallions whom a woman stirs up at her own risk and expense. The young woman who encounters a horny young man and does not immediately flee has only herself to blame for any loss of virtue that ensues.

There is nothing unusual about this belief. In South America, in Mediterranean countries and in most of the Third World it is the rule, not the exception. Here in Canada, the self-proclaimed "multicultural" society, one might have expected such an article to stimulate intense debate over the persistence of this cultural assumption. The article, though poorly composed and of low-level insight, taken as a *symptom*, presented a rare opportunity to discuss deep-seated beliefs with tragic consequences today, in a rational manner.

Prominent Christians, Jews and Moslems might have placed the issue in a theological context; a sociologist might have discussed changes in Canadian mating habits; a psychologist might have described the mental processes common to men who exploit and degrade women. After all, this occurred at a university, where such human resources are handy, and on tenure. The incident could have focused the campus on one of its most urgent problems—and God only knows university people love to talk about sex.

What was the administration's response? They denounced the article and suspended the professor. Case closed.

In one public gesture, they washed their hands of any responsibility for the situation, took symbolic revenge on behalf of "victims," and "sent a signal" to any potential "abuser" on campus who harbours similar views:

Shut up.

In the dream world of symbolic language, when we are unwilling or unable to face a problem, we deal with it by "sending out a signal." As unaddressed problems pile up in the real world, these signals multiply until authorities are so occupied with "sending out a signal," they have lost the ability to *do* anything.

When I attended the University of British Columbia, a "flasher" who had been exposing himself to women in the library stacks was apprehended after several complaints. The University response? They confiscated his library card. Yet a library card was not necessary to enter the library at the time. The punishment did not prevent him from exposing himself in the stacks—only from borrowing the books.

A Window of Opportunity

Metaphors are magical things, binding the world together in unpredictable ways, implicitly hinting at a oneness (whatever that means) to everything. But once exposed to the open air, metaphors have a given shelf life, a "best before" date, after which they begin to go rotten.

There is a sense in which all words are metaphors. Take an everyday, seemingly concrete noun like, say, *chair*.

Of course, theoretically, the word *chair* once referred to a specific chair, the first chair, before which everybody sat on the floor. But it cannot have taken many chairs before the word *chair* came to signify, not a specific chair, but anything you sat on that had four legs and a back. *Chair* by that point meant, as it were, "chairness."

As an indication of "chairness," the word *chair* had lost some, though not all, of its original meaning—a gap easily filled with a modifier or two, as in "*kitchen* chair," to haul the word back to its original function as a description of something specific in the world. All you had to do was tell people what kind of chair it was, and they would be able to point one out.

As it lost meaning, however, the word *chair* gained in its potential for metaphorical and emotional content. Expressions such as "Mr. Chairman" developed—with the word *chair* conferring a feeling of dignity, authority and order. *Chair* became, in part, a metaphor for the feelings of relief and security that usually accompany the act of sitting down: Pull up a chair. Sit down. Take a load off your feet.

When we use the expression, "Pull up a chair," we are not specifically asking the listener to carry an item of furniture, but rather to relax, to drop his guard in a receptive and friendly atmosphere. In this sense, the original meaning of the word *chair*, as an indication of a specific physical object, has receded into the background.

Having reached this metaphorical stage, the word *chair* is now ripe, bursting with emotional juice, ready to be picked and put to manipulative use. It is not difficult to imagine a politician on television talking his way out of a thorny situation by using the word *chair* in an expression such as, "We have asked the opposing sides to take a chair and look at the problem"—implying a leisurely but concentrated discussion, in much the same way as the word *table* is used to imply level-headed negotiation, as in, "We will bring these issues to the *table*."

Of course, *chair* has not yet ripened to this point; but *table* certainly has, just as *window* ripened as a metaphor during the 1980s in the expression, "window of opportunity." During the Free Trade debates, *window* in this sense became useful as a way to evoke the invigourating fresh air of global competition, as opposed to the stale claustrophobia of protectionism; as a release or escape (the implied window is open, not shut), together with a sense of urgency—for a window can slam shut at any moment, on your fingers perhaps.

Today, although *window* has gone slightly rancid, we still have a bumper crop of symbolic language to choose from: *abuse* (disgust), *racism* (hatred and contempt), *in place* (exactness and precision), *impact* (dynamic forcefulness), *choice* (democratic tolerance), *care* (friendship and concern), *at the end of the day* (benign completion), *community* (humane fellowship), *hopefully* (optimism and sincerity): The list goes on and on.

Whole news clips, speeches and elections are constructed of these expressions, like strips of print cut from magazines by blackmailers, pasted into sentences whose origins in the real world are impossible to trace. It is possible to argue for hours on a topic, without saying a thing.

Analogue and Digital

The most treacherous metaphors are those we use to envisage and describe the work of the brain itself, as it accumulates and sorts data, makes decisions about the nature of reality, and initiates a course of action. This is a dicey business, for the brain's conception of itself, like a snake swallowing its tail, eventually comes up against an impossibility. Whether as a soul or a chemistry set, any picture we make of the brain is bound to be dead wrong.

Popular metaphors describing the brain's activity tend to follow current external developments in technology. We like to think of the mind as a state-of-the-art organ, a subtle postmodern miracle and not the primordial, squishy mass of cells it physically appears to be.

32

Thus, in the nineteenth century, the mind was described in terms of the steam engine—as a powerful boiler operating under pressure, which, should it accumulate too great a "head of steam," could "blow its stack." Safety valves were thus required at all times—alcohol, laudanum and cocaine. With the development of the electric motor, the blown stack became a short circuit in which "wires became crossed" and a person had a "nervous breakdown," like an appliance on the fritz. Devices were therefore needed to lower the amount of current—such as Valium and Librium.

Today we imagine the mind as a computer—a complicated assembly of interconnected memory units, whose path is navigated by millions of binary switches—forks in the information highway where one of two choices can and must be made. After a series of either-or intersections made at blinding speed, we eventually come to a decision.

The obvious advantage to this binary, digital model of the brain is that it provides a traceable pathway for an institution to replicate: By following this pattern in decision-making, successful mental pathways can be repeated, failures avoided, and some of the guesswork can be taken out of corporate living.

The disadvantage to the computer model of the mind is that individuals who embrace it in real life are apt to try to think in digital stages, in terms of a "yes or no" response to one isolated observation or decision at a time—neglecting the mind's *analogue* capacity to scan any situation as a whole.

Analogue formats—clocks, speedometers, compasses and the like—display the whole picture, together with an indicator pointing to our current position. The movement of a needle on a dial indicates trends and nuances that make life a continuous process and not a series of stops and starts. We prefer analogue watches and speedometers because they tell us not only the time or the speed, but also where our action fits in an overall scheme: how fast the car can go, whether it is speeding up or slowing down, how much time we have to get there.

If we apply the analogue dial as a metaphor for other areas of life, we discover a relativist world in which the current trend in an overall scheme is as important as the indicator's current position on the dial.

Digital formats, on the other hand, describe a binary choice: on or off, one or zero, yes or no, in a series of static situations and not in the context of a continuous movement. In digital time it is noon, then it is not. In digital speed, you are either going sixty miles an hour or you are going sixty-one. The movement between sixty and sixty-one does not exist.

When we apply the digital model to real life we create an imaginary world of heroes and villains, win and lose, good and bad, up and down. In the digital world, the words *villain* and *hero* describe two entirely different people; a villain is not simply a hero on a bad day.

Both metaphors, analogue and digital, are necessary to envisage the world. Disease, for example, is best described in analogue terms, since the progress of a disease—better or worse—is at least as important as our condition at the moment. Death, on the other hand, is digital; one is either dead or one is not. There is no room to manoeuvre, and one must simply accept the situation as it is.

By the same token, sex is analogue, while pregnancy is digital. A broken arm is analogue; a lost arm is digital. A hockey game is analogue; the final score is digital.

All rather fun, but a good deal depends on discerning which is which.

In 1992, the Canadian government committed a landmark act of digital-analogue confusion when it tried to express the constitution of the country, a relative, analogue item if there ever was one, in a digital format—as a yes-no referendum. The result was a national fiasco.

Our news media, craving simplicity and in a chronic panic to produce copy on time, habitually express life in digital terms. Abortion and euthanasia: right or wrong? Will Quebec stay or go? Is the economy in good shape or in bad shape? Is this athlete, movie star or politician a winner or a loser?

The correct answer to all these questions could easily be "both," but the digital format will not allow for this. As a result, discussion on such topics ricochets between two wrong answers, over and over, like a computer called upon to find the square root of *pi*.

Thugs

The radio program *Sunday Morning*, one of Canada's most revered sources of weekly news analysis, recently ran an item about some unpleasant events in Moser River, Nova Scotia. It seems that after the RCMP closed the local constabulary, the village was terrorized by local "thugs," destroying property and intimidating innocent citizens. The situation became front page news when a local man was murdered.

Following an attack on his ten-year-old son, the man rammed the alleged attacker's car. RCMP officers from the next town, arriving too late to assess the situation accurately, arrested the "victim" along with the "thugs." While in jail the man was beaten to death. One of the "thugs" was charged with the murder.

Hardly a high point in Canadian law enforcement, but nothing spectacular when compared with, say, the Montreal police shooting of an innocent Haitian motorist who had obediently stopped at a red light. Every year, citizens die thanks to bungling by the police. In Canada, far more misery is caused by incompetence than by conscious evil.

But the *Sunday Morning* piece took the standard format. Determined to maximize drama and human interest, the item described the plight of Moser River against the evil force in the community, together with a sympathetic profile of the murdered man and the anguish of his family and friends. We heard excerpts from a town meeting in which villagers vented their fury at mortified representatives of the provincial government and the RCMP.

A member of a local citizens' group described to the interviewer the experience of having been beaten with hockey sticks. A clergyman castigated authorities for allowing the situation to continue.

A prime example of an analogue, human event crammed into a digital format.

The story, as told, assumed the binary form of a professional wrestling bout, in which the good guys who obey the rules face off against the bad guys who break them, mediated by ineffective referees who always seem to have their backs turned whenever the bad guy administers a choke hold or a trunk-grab. Should the good guy, after unbearable provocation and frustration, run amok and resort to a few illegal moves himself, who can blame him? Indeed, who can resist cheering him on?

Like a professional wrestling announcer, the CBC journalist placed herself firmly on the side of the good guys and against the bad guys (depersonalized by the use of false names, and by the generic word "thug"), and shared the spectators' contempt for the referees. Finally, in tones as ritualistic as a benediction, she concurred with a series of good guy witnesses that Something Must Be Done.

The key to this story is the word *thug*, used about twelve times to describe the source of the violence—in fact, the miscreants were never characterized in any other way. The word was chosen from the thesaurus with care and reiterated like a mantra, in order to disguise with emotion an utter absence of fact in the report.

Dating back to the British occupation of India, the word *thug* refers to a militant, violent religious sect which the Imperial army managed to suppress—no doubt with equal violence—in 1835. As a means of quasi-racial demonization, the term has a proud colonial heritage when used to describe incorrigible people who engage in criminal brutality.

But in real life, who were these "thugs" of Moser River? Where did they come from? Were they vacationing Mafiosi from New York? Skinheads from Berlin? For all we were told, they could have come from another planet.

Most likely, they were native sons who sprang straight out of the society they terrorized.

Even assuming that they were local, were they young or old, employed or unemployed? Who were their parents? If they were men—and we must presume so, for there was no indication either way—did they have wives or girlfriends? Where did they live? Did they rent or own? What did they wear? Were their nocturnal rampages fueled with alcohol and drugs? If so, who sold these substances to them?

Did the fact that they beat people with hockey sticks indicate that they were hockey players? For what team?

The more one thought about the situation as described, the less one knew. In an interview early in the piece, an ex-RCMP officer from the area went so far as to indicate that the murder victim, while an upright citizen at the time of his death, was not always so virtuous—in fact one received the distinct impression that he may once have been a "thug" himself.

The story of Moser River provided a fascinating opportunity to examine the culture of small town violence in Canada, to look directly at the rage that seems to lurk just beneath the surface of idle, young, rural men—a rage that has existed since well before *Sunday Morning* switched on its tape recorder.

As a dance musician I saw it on the faces of young men in New Glasgow and Sydney, sometimes shortly before having my eyes blackened just for the fun of it. In Truro I once saw a young man's face rendered unrecognizable by blows from his own guitar. At a dance near Moncton, a young man was kicked to death, while at the IOOF Hall in Stellarton, someone was stabbed. In Pictou, a naval officer was beaten so badly that he lost an eye. I knew a young man who was known to grab an opponent's rib cage and break the sternum. You could hear the snap from some distance away.

There is a trick they do in Pictou County: Young men drive slowly on a two-lane highway until somebody tries to pass them, then they speed up abruptly, stranding the passing car in the left lane that faces oncoming traffic, forcing the terrified driver to choose between a head-on collision and the ditch. (A powerful metaphor for continental free trade perhaps, but I doubt if that is what they have in mind.)

In Eastern Europe, such chaps form enthusiastic local militias, taking out their frustrations on competing ethnic groups. In Canada, they beat people up with hockey sticks.

These fellows are not criminals in the usual sense of the word—unless they are caught. Most go on to become law-abiding if frequently alcoholic citizens. They marry (Heaven help their wives), have children (spare the rod and spoil the child), hold down jobs and worry about the crime rate.

Clearly, violence is not always a product of American TV. There is such a thing as Canadian violence, with its own ancient origins, expressed in its own characteristic style. Brutality is part of Canadian culture too.

But we fail to bring this up in our media. Too complicated. Too relativist and ironic. Too Canadian. Better stick to the good guys-bad guys format, with a cast of victims, thugs and bumbling referees. This is the dream the audience prefers. This is what they want to hear.

A World of Our Own

The simultaneous triumph and death of a metaphor occurs when the dream world it creates is taken for reality and treated as such. When that point is reached, the metaphor is no longer an imaginative tool but a successful fraud.

Where it once illuminated the real world, the metaphor now hides reality as the basis for decisions and actions. Where it once focused the real world into an unexpected and pleasing unity, the metaphor now tears it apart into little, private fantasies. When a word like *crime* or *victim* empties of meaning and fills with the unique imagery of individual fears, we can talk about crimes and victims all we like, but no two of us will ever be talking about the same thing.

Canada is not something we experience in the town hall or the village square anymore, with the town band playing in the gazebo; it is something we watch on television, read about in newspapers and magazines, and hear on the radio. For most people, Canada has become an electronic magazine stand, an accumulation of arbitrarily juxtaposed images and random details, both fact and fiction, some local but most imported from other parts of Canada, from America, and from no place at all. Yet our magazines and TV shows carry no warning label—no designation as "Fact" or "Fiction," "From Here" or "From There." We can never be certain which is which.

And the issues follow suit. Crime? The Canadian concept of crime is a blend of American statistics, urban myth, TV shows, and whichever foreign atrocity happens to have hopped onto the CP Wireservice during the last twenty-four hours—with a few familiar names thrown in to concretize the mix.

The Canadian family? An odd mental creation—a deconstructive social critique based on notions derived from *Father Knows Best,* Christian evangelical rants, Sylvia Plath nightmares and *The Drunkard,* together with our own uniquely unhappy families and the perceived happiness or unhappiness of other families in our particular car pool.

Relations between Canada and Quebec? To Quebec, Canada is an Alberta politician in aviator glasses, and a queue of elderly Ontarians in acrylic doubleknits stomping on the Quebec flag. To English Canada, Quebec is a syrup farmer in a toque, a dead body in a car trunk, and a gun-happy police officer, together with a personal restaurant experience while motoring to the Maritimes one summer, several years ago.

Sometimes I think each of us lives in a soundproof, curved media bubble. We try to look at each other, but see only distorted gesticulating shapes. We try to read each other's lips, knowing that it may not even be a real person on the other side—it may be our own reflection.

The current debates raging in Canada over our institutions and values are in a sense clashes of metaphor, bubbles bumping against one another then slipping away. We compare dreams, each convinced that only his dream is real, then we shrug our shoulders and it all floats away.

I wonder if we will ever get around to talking about real life again.

THE IRON PEOPLE AND
THE EARTH PEOPLE:
A TRAIL OF CROSSED SIGNALS

I grew up in a town that offered a minimum of contact between the dominant, colonial culture and those of other ethnic groups. The implied assumption was that, having scrambled to a higher plateau, my ethnic group had nothing to gain and everything to lose by making contact with these retrograde life forms, which posed an ongoing threat to the level of civilization we had achieved. We were not unique in this belief, which continues to be held by dominant cultures from London to Tokyo.

Nor were we avid followers of Rousseau when it came to the "natural man." To the traditional Scots Protestant, mankind was seen as inherently evil, goodness was something that had to be taught, and salvation was attained through hard work and self-denial. "Natural man" did not embody uncorrupted innocence but rather a kind of treacherous animal cunning, a savage charm to beguile the unwary and drag him back to the stone age.

Things are no doubt seen differently back home today; but when I grew up, civilization was at a precarious stage, barely holding on with its fingernails.

Despite this tacit feeling of peril, I managed to make intermittent contact with other ethnic groups in the area—everyone but the Micmac Indians. Although I lived two miles from the reservation, I never met a Micmac in my life.

The Micmac nation lived just outside town by the Trans-Canada highway. (I have since noticed that highways, power lines and other unpleasant utilities have a way of passing straight through reservations.) On its way to Halifax our speeding car passed the Glooscap Trading Post, a wooden replica of a *tipi* where pastel baskets were sold to tourists. Nearby stood a series of dwellings; most were ordinary prefab bungalows, yet these homes were not placed on the lot, nor were they manicured, like similar houses in town. None seemed to come equipped with a front doorstep, nor did their owners own a lawn mower. There were no flower gardens.

These people were different from us—a difference of unknown extent.

If Truro's white protestant self-isolation implied some threat to be warded off, then the existence and placement of the reservation, the fact that its citizens did not even attend the same schools or walk the same streets, suggested that the Micmac must present the greatest danger of all to us.

This impression was vividly reinforced in history class, where we learned about unfortunate Jesuit priests who fell victim to Iroquois torture. Unlike nebulous references to European war atrocities and Inquisition torture methods, these were lovingly-detailed nightmares of boiling water, red-hot sticks and severed digits. History was further brought to life in schoolyard games of cowboys and Indians, and by watching Technicolor movies in which innocent settlers were pierced with arrows, strung up by their heels over slow-burning fires, and buried in anthills under the boiling sun.

Literature provided yet another source of information about the Indian threat. In *Tom Sawyer*, the evil menace at the church picnic, the villain to be feared, is not the negro as one might think, given the novel's southern setting, but "Injun Joe"—a bloodthirsty, demented savage who threatens Tom and Becky with murder at the very least.

If *Huckleberry Finn* is suspect on school curricula for its treatment of Jim the slave, why not *Tom Sawyer* for its treatment of Injun Joe?

Every Canadian of European descent over the age of thirty has in a hundred different ways been trained to believe that the Native Indian is a menace—even when facts proclaim the situation to be precisely the other way around. Although newspapers abound with horror stories of systemic child abuse in residential schools, of desperate poverty and a suicide epidemic among northern teenagers, still in the cellars of our memory lurk powerful, vivid images of tortured priests, slaughtered settlers, of Injun Joe pursuing Tom and Becky in that dark cave. That is how racial hatred works.

While it would require a degree of paranoia to suspect a consciously induced campaign of disinformation, still one wonders: If some fiendish social engineer were to have designed a program to explain and justify the systematic extermination of a race of people, could they have done it better?

For genocide to occur, whether against Indians, Gypsies, Jews or Zulu, the victim must be feared. Evil is rarely a conscious undertaking. Most oppressors do their work in the sincere belief that it is *they* who are the innocent victims.

Regardless of national origin, Canadians are still terrified of the Native Indian. How else could it have been possible for the Oka Crisis of 1990 to develop as it did; for *le Sûreté de Québec* to launch a military assault with automatic weapons and concussion grenades, then for Premier Bourassa to call in the Canadian Army under General John de Chastelain with tanks and helicopters—all to defend us against forty Mohawks? Surely no sane country could have permitted such an escalation to occur unless it was drawing from deep wells of subliminal fear—especially given that the issue of contention was an area of sacred land, subject to a land claims negotiation, about to be clear-cut in order to expand a municipal golf course. A *golf course!*

Today, the episode reads like something out of *Dr. Strangelove*: The army of a democratic middle power, a member of the G7 with a reputation for peacekeeping, stands ready to do battle against forty Natives in a tense, armed confrontation, lines drawn, that goes on for months—and for what? To defend the right of a French-Canadian town to have wider access to the Scottish national sport!

Really, sometimes multiculturalism can go too far.

And the madness was not limited to the participants themselves. Other than as a mass hallucination, how is it possible to explain the media's reporting of the Crisis—which was about as factual as *The Last of the Mohicans?* How were respected journalists from *La Presse* and *The Globe and Mail* persuaded that the tiny Kanehsatake Native community had, out of the blue, sprouted entire battalions of anonymous terrorists made up of hardened criminals and Vietnam commandos, equipped with a state-of-the-art military arsenal and with—here it becomes truly surrealistic—*Mafia connections?*

As with the John F. Kennedy assassination, when faced with incomprehensible events it is tempting to concoct elaborate scenarios involving a conscious high-level plan: that the Oka Crisis was a pretext for the government of Quebec to demonize and then to crush the movement for Native sovereignty, during a period of delicate constitutional negotiations with Ottawa. But had such a Machiavellian plan existed, could its execution have been so incompetent?

Well, as a matter of fact it could. Canadian police performance traditionally contains a good deal of *Three Stooges* material in the repertoire. One recalls the slapstick tactics undertaken by the RCMP against the FLQ in the late '60s—all those pointless barn-burnings, bungled burglaries and inept frame-ups.

Indeed, the Oka version of the Charge of the Light Brigade, resulting in the death of Corporal LeMay, recalls an earlier instance of Quebec law enforcement in which a SWAT team, out to nab a suspected bank robber, charged a motel room in the middle of the night and riddled it with bullets, only to find that they had killed an innocent carpet-layer sleeping in his bed. Not that this sort of nonsense is peculiar to Quebec: In cities all across the land, police weapons display an alarming tendency to misfire, especially in the presence of minority races.

But no conspiracy theory explains the bug-eyed credulousness of ordinary Canadians, French and English; the fact that, in 1990, millions of adult, literate people were ready to believe in monsters named "Lasagna" and "Noriega," that a secret army had been raised in a Montreal suburb, large and well-armed enough to justify mobilizing the Canadian army—over a *golf course.*

It appears to me far more likely that the Oka Crisis was another product of a vivid collective nightmare inspired by a fairy tale out of the Brothers Grimm: a tale of two imaginary nations, of tragic misunderstandings that began centuries ago with a diabolical combination of bad timing, crossed signals and sheer bad luck.

Space Travel

Friday, August 3, 1492: Three vehicles embark from what they understand to be the centre of civilization, to venture beyond the boundaries of the known universe. Although these ships display the flag of Spain, its Italian captain and multinational crew collectively represent a technologically-advanced warrior culture we will call the *Iron People*.

The launching was conceived on the theory that space, over distance, can warp to the point where it turns back on itself and West becomes East. The notion is controversial: 8,800 people were burnt at the stake over a twenty-year period for harbouring similarly contentious ideas. It is characteristic of the Iron People to favour an authoritarian culture in which knowledge is carefully managed to support the dominant world view.

The leading ship carries letters from the King and Queen of Spain to the Grand Kahn of Cathay. Interpreters on board speak Hebrew, Chaldean and Arabic. The explorers are confident. They believe they have covered every eventuality. And they are wrong.

Friday, October 12, 1492: Three space vehicles alight on what they believe to be the southern tip of the continent of Asia, known as the Indies. Upon landing, however, they unexpectedly encounter another technologically-advanced warrior culture hitherto unknown to them. Labouring under the illusion that they have reached Asia, they refer to these people as "Indians."

These "Indians," although divided into many nations, collectively represent a broad-based culture we will call, for the sake of simplicity and clarity, the *Earth People*.

Other, similar voyages follow. Gradually it dawns upon European visitors that this is not Asia but a world totally new to them, a terrifying world of hazardous rivers, precipitous cliffs and impenetrable forests, populated by life forms never before seen— moose, skunk, mosquito, raccoon, caribou, buffalo, opossum and rattlesnake. But strangest of all to European explorers is the imaginary world of the Earth People.

It is fundamental to the Iron People to regard goodness and truth as static qualities of an unchanging, one and only Supreme Being, and to see change as a symptom of falsehood, deception and evil. The spiritual universe of the Earth People, on the other hand, is not static but eternally mutating, populated by a bewildering gallery of tricksters and transformers who constantly change themselves and the universe from one thing into another.

The existence of this new world, antithetical to Europe both materially and spiritually, is a time bomb of potential doubt threatening the accepted truths of the Iron People: Is Europe not the centre of the universe? Do other cultures feel themselves to inhabit the centre of the universe as well? If indeed we are God's chosen people, then why would He create a world so different from ours? Is truth not absolute but relative?

So contrary are the two world views, neither provides a reliable yardstick with which to measure the other. From the first contact each culture forms a distorting lens through which they exchange views. In Northern British Columbia, one of the Earth People describes an incoming Spanish ship as "an island with three trees, covered with crows: when one of the crows calls out, the others climb to the top of the trees." Captain James Cook, meanwhile, interprets their ceremonial dance of welcome as "...truly frightful. He worked himself into the highest frenzy, uttering something between a howl and a song."

But the long-term effects of such distortions are not apparent, as long as interaction with the Earth People in northern North America is limited to European fur traders—representatives of an emerging mercantile class who, like the Earth People, are mobile, value the ownership of resources over land, and are trained to function in a barter economy.

A flourishing trade develops, thanks to these practical similarities, and to differences in technological and economic development that cause each side to view their own goods as worthless and common, and those they receive as rare prizes. Yet, although the Earth People may value iron fish hooks more than the pelts of sea otters, they reveal themselves to be canny businessmen, travelling from one vessel to another for competing offers, and establishing special trading areas where visitors are compelled to bid directly against one another, thus raising prices to the maximum.

Despite their expertise, their technological sophistication, and the high prices fetched for furs in Europe and Asia, it takes a skilled European trader to avoid bankruptcy doing business with the Earth People.

A delicate balance is achieved as both sides of the trading relationship adapt to the other according to their perceived self-interest, always with one thing in common—the mutual quest for profit. When one side undergoes a cultural change in the direction of the other culture, as when traders don buckskins, or when a band of trappers moves their village closer to a trading fort, such changes are voluntary and self-directed, not compelled by the other.

Underlying cultural conflicts between the Earth People and the Iron People will not become evident as long as the trading of fur takes precedence over the trading of ideas.

Then permanent settlers begin to arrive from Europe—sedentary, agricultural refugees displaced by religious persecution and by feudal land grabs—and it becomes evident how deeply antithetical the two world views really are. To make things worse, it dawns on settlers that they and their families are here for life, physically committed to the unfathomable terrain of the Earth People.

Culture shock sets in, then a kind of panic as settlers frantically scramble to establish zones of familiar physical and spiritual territory—cutting down trees, planting crops, building churches, schools and fences.

But it is the spiritual differences between the two peoples that cause the most trouble. If I fail to comprehend your world view, it means that I cannot predict what you will do in a hypothetical situation. Will we agree on fundamental issues of good and evil, right and wrong? Will your world view permit you to hurt me with a clear conscience?

Crossed Signals

It is difficult to imagine two more inimical world views than those of the Earth People and the Iron People; the fact that these two cultures come together during a period of European turmoil—political, spiritual and economic—under circumstances guaranteed to produce maximum dislocation on both sides, can only be regarded as perverse coincidence.

The two cultures cannot see eye-to-eye on issues as basic as time itself. The Earth People are utterly mystified by the clock, which settlers seem to regard as far more than a machine. To the Iron People, every glance at the dial is a tiny religious experience in which time is harnessed to human will, rendered visible and measurable. When time is measured in hours and minutes, eternity ceases to dominate everyday life, days do not get longer and shorter with the seasons, and age and death seem less inevitable and poignant. As well, measured time is not something human beings share with other creatures: It is not necessary to synchronize one's watch with other animals and with nature. The clock thereby reinforces mankind's view of itself as separate and above nature, as an exceptional being placed on this earth to órganize the universe on God's behalf.

None of this makes any sense to the Earth People, who cannot understand why anyone would want such a machine.

And in the new world, they are right. Gradually and reluctantly, settlers must face the fact that their precious clock, vital as it may be for the smooth running of a European city, is of no use whatsoever. It reveals nothing about crucial changes in weather, temperature or the amount of light available; nor does the clock's extension, the calendar, supply information about when to plant crops, when to fish—or indeed any insights relevant to daily life in this part of the world.

The more they learn about the new world and the Earth People, the more threatened the Iron People feel.

Earth People do not envisage time as separate from events or from the motion of nature, nor do they have an external device for suspending personal judgements about the relative importance of things—in order to be "on time" in an abstract, absolute sense. This is a source of constant annoyance to the Iron People, for whom to be "on time" is a moral imperative in itself.

The two peoples will never see eye to eye on the issue of time. To the Iron People, the Earth People will always seem tardy and untrustworthy, while to the Earth People the Iron People will seem compulsive and obsessed with a machine.

But the most pernicious breakdowns in communication between the two peoples are those that occur in ordinary, everyday conversation.

Every human dialogue follows the same pattern: Person A opens the conversation, to which Person B replies briefly, giving A permission to continue. A then talks on a chosen topic until finished; then he pauses. This pause is B's chance either to speak his mind, or to remain silent; should he remain silent, A is then free to set the conversational agenda once more, and a new round begins.

This format occurs in all cultures, over a campfire, a table or telephone lines.

But the timing differs from one culture to another. The pause that a European takes to allow B his chance to speak is, on average, three seconds shorter than the pause a Native Indian requires—a subtle but crucial difference, for it means that, in conversation with a European, the Native can never get a word in edgewise, while to the European, the Native seems chronically sullen and uncommunicative.

Other subliminal messages between the two groups are similarly ripe for misunderstandings. In a meeting between two people of unequal status, the Earth People traditionally regard it as incumbent upon the party with higher status to offer a gift, a symbol of his preeminent position. By accepting this gift, the recipient accedes to the superiority of the other and the transaction is complete. To the Iron People on the other hand, giving a gift is not a ritual to establish a hierarchy, but an act of communion between equals, requiring either a return gift or an acknowledgement in the form of thanks. Because of this difference, whether as an openhanded gift or as charity, neither party can give or receive a gift without appearing rude to the other.

When two cultures differ on the meaning of basic social signals, coexistence is impossible unless one side gives in to the other. And to their dismay, settlers find that in order to acquire food and shelter, they have no choice but to convert to the worldview of the Earth People—an implicit spiritual surrender which they resent and determine to keep to a minimum.

Although they may now tell time by the sun and not the clock, the Iron People at the same time set about to convert natives to their world view in other ways—if only to balance the books and to ease their own fear.

Witches and Demons

Predictably, the most dangerous conflicts between the two cultures centre around religious practices and the ethics they convey. To the Iron People, with no religious paradigm other than European Christian imagery, the religion of the Earth People is nothing but superstition, and the activities of the native shaman are those of a witch.

Unlike a priest, the shaman does not simply pray to the Great Spirit, but shares some of His power for good and evil. Furthermore, the shaman's power extends into secular areas as he performs political, medical and judicial functions in the community. To the Iron People, the religious figure the shaman resembles most is the rebel angel—who, not content to cede power to God, reigns over a parallel spiritual universe called Hell. In the mythology of the Iron People, the native shaman becomes a symbol of the Devil himself.

Neither do the Earth People appreciate the rituals of Roman Catholicism—even though the Jesuits offer such concessions as declaring the beaver a fish so that it can be eaten during Lent. They cannot understand why a soul would be treated any better or worse after death than it was treated in life; in fact, they find this concern with death and the afterlife rather morbid, and do not respond enthusiastically to the threat of eternal torture.

Belief systems beget ethical systems, and here the gap widens further. To the Iron People it is wrong to lie, to steal, or to go back on one's word; to the Earth People it is wrong to name the dead, to harm a guest, and especially to rob a grave. Soon both sides form stereotypes of each other based on their differing versions of good and evil. The Iron People regard the Earth People as liars and thieves; the Earth People regard the Iron People as vampires— reinforced by the fact that, in their mythology, the Devil often appears as a white boy.

As the land begins to fill up with settlers, the differences between the two peoples become more and more acute. Earth People base their concept of property on resources: You may wander wherever you wish, but you must not fish from a stream whose trout belong to another family. The Iron People, on the other hand, fence in squares of land for themselves regardless of what it contains, which is as incomprehensible to the Earth People as it would be to own squares of the sea or the air.

To the Iron People, a civilized person lives by gardens, a barbarian by pastures, and a savage by hunting and fishing. Thus, the Earth People appear as savages, no matter how civilized their behavior. Settlers on the *Mayflower*, having arrived too late in the year to plant the crops for which they have seeds, survive only because the Earth People supply them with corn, which grows fast enough to produce a crop before winter. But no amount of friendliness will ease the moral and spiritual gap between them.

To settlers, the Earth People evoke old resentments, reminding them of people they do not like—the lords who oppressed peasants and drove them from home. Free from work, Earth People wander the forest as though they owned it, hunting game at will. Some of their tents bear an uncanny resemblance to gentlemen's summer houses. Like scions of the European upper classes, natives are sexually active in their teens, sire children outside Holy Matrimony and display an indecent amount of physical vanity. (During epidemics of smallpox, large numbers commit suicide rather than bear disfiguring pock marks on their faces.)

But what terrifies the Iron People most is the prospect that they themselves might one day become Earth People and become part of that terrible wilderness—a chaos they associate with Hell itself; that they might "descend to the level of savages." This deep-seated fear of savagery goes back to the Romans, maintaining their civilization against the onslaught of barbarians at the gates.

The physical attractiveness of the athletic Earth People makes them all the more threatening as a seductive trap, the Devil's lure. Laws are passed imposing heavy fines for gambling, fornication, long hair, bare breasts, polygamy, body-greasing and even "conspicuous mourning."

An Endangered Species

Whether intentionally or not, when two cultures meet they teach one another; and despite the efforts of the Iron People to insulate themselves it is the Earth People who do most of the teaching. After all, this is their environment. They have been here for centuries.

For sheer comfort and practicality, Iron People wear moccasins, which are quieter for hunting and dry more quickly than boots. The native hunting shirt proves so popular that it becomes a symbol of the American Revolution. Gradually the Iron People—especially those who live outside town—begin to look and act more and more like Earth People.

During continual French-English skirmishes in New England and Upper and Lower Canada, complicated alliances are struck with the Earth People by both sides. Both armies discover that the native system of battle, which resembles what will become known as guerilla warfare, is more effective than the field battles favoured by the Iron People. Imitating the Earth People becomes a matter of survival on the battlefield as well as in the wilderness.

Iron People now routinely use toboggans, snowshoes, canoes, tobacco, maple sugar, corn and wild rice. They imitate local fishing techniques and adopt into their language words like chipmunk, muskeg, maize, skunk and raccoon. Many adopt native marriages and sexual mores. Clerics complain that, as they travel farther from population centres, the two peoples become indistinguishable.

It will never be known how many Iron People actually become Earth People. Such people disappear into the wilderness and, having adopted an oral culture, leave no historical tracks. However, estimates of the rate of conversion can be made by referring to records of captivity during the French-Iroquois wars: For every two captives ransomed or exchanged, one prefers to remain among the Earth People. Yet there exists not one example of an Iroquois, by choice, joining the other society.

The Earth People know how to educate without physical punishment, how to teach by example, how to convert enemies. To the Iron People, a steady pattern of cultural capitulation comes to represent the ultimate victory of the Devil over God on this earth.

In the New England fishing village of Marblehead in 1762, a group of women set upon two native prisoners from Maine and literally tear them apart with their bare hands. The women are on their way home from church.

Now we begin to see some of the emotional intensity and the pent-up rage that characterized the Oka Crisis of 1990.

So terrified have the Iron People become, they begin a conscious effort to transform the entire landscape into something more familiar, into towns, farms, pastures—and golf courses. Tragically, this effort involves removing the Earth People onto "reserves." Again in history we see the oppressed imitating their oppressors as the Iron People, having been driven from their ancestral lands in Europe and expelled by brute force, inflict the same oppressive conditions upon the Earth People.

A poisonous confusion becomes a permanent institution, administered by something called the Department of Indian Affairs. Contact, in the sense of a trade of objects and ideas, ceases. With neither side any closer to understanding the other, the two peoples are doomed to fear and incomprehension. Tragedy is inevitable, as the mistakes of the first contact are repeated, over and over again.

Yet, as their cultural dominance takes its toll on the environment, as their ethical system loses cohesion and as the suffering of the Earth People becomes an increasing source of shame, the Iron People become uneasy victors indeed. A "revolution in electronic communication" has the dual effect of creating a sense of solidarity among Earth People, while fragmenting the Iron People by asserting the relativity of any world view.

One culture weakens despite its wealth and its weapons of war, while the other gains strength, despite poverty and despair. And a constitutional accord crumbles when an Indian raises a feather in Manitoba.

Out of the Woods

A few years ago I delivered one of my periodic rants on the state of the national psyche to a cultural conference at the University of British Columbia, attended by, among others, a number of First Nations groups. The lecture hall was large and florescent, one of those bear-pit arrangements in which the speaker stands at a dais on the floor and speaks to an audience seated on risers tiered above him.

As I wound up my question-and-answer finale to the half-empty hall, I noticed him standing over to one side in front of the audience, waiting patiently for me to finish: a good-looking, deeply-tanned man of medium height, with neatly-combed greying hair, wearing a windbreaker and a sports shirt with a button-down collar. He looked like an ex-athlete. He could have been the coach of a minor league baseball team.

I thanked the audience and received my little spatter of applause. Just as I was gathering my notes to leave, he stepped to centre stage, smiled at the audience and began to speak, with the authority of an official from a sponsoring organization whose job it is to thank the guest speaker and present him with a token gift.

But there was no sponsoring organization; nor were speakers at the conference to receive gifts.

I exchanged puzzled glances with my audience, who seemed not to recognize him either. Even so, the man's sheer confidence convinced us to settle down and listen to whatever he had to say.

Without introducing or explaining himself in any way, he told the following tale:

Thousands of years ago there was a prophecy that a people from another culture would come to this continent. They would come bearing a cross, which would be pictured either with or without a circle around it. If the cross was circled, there would be harmony between the two cultures; if it was not circled, there would be nothing but trouble for five hundred years.

However, this trouble would one day come to an end. The first sign of the coming renewal would be the appearance of seven "philosophers"—a word synonymous with "artist" in native languages—who would introduce a new regard for the land. A century later, hundreds of other "philosophers" would appear bearing the same message of redemption.

The man then turned to me and smiled with perfect teeth: "You are part of that. You with your big mouth."

With that, he presented me with a calendar containing reproductions of pictures by the Group of Seven, then shook my hand, and walked out of the auditorium.

I never saw him again. To this day, I have no idea who he was.

THE HIDDEN PEOPLE:
ENJOYING THE INCOGNITO LIFESTYLE

Down in the Dumps

Uncle Roy stood well over six feet, easily the tallest in the family, with thinning red hair, a long, big-boned face and huge hands. A naturally funny man with a slow Maritime drawl and a big bark of a laugh, Roy liked to tell rambling, poker-faced shaggy dog stories. He kept a pint of rum hidden in the horse barn out of Aunt Ella's sight, "in case of an emergency." He regularly took the village children on sleigh rides in winter, and in an old fire truck in summer. He was a member of the volunteer fire department. He loved to sing baritone in barbershop quartets, in church choirs and in impromptu recitals in the barn.

Then Roy suffered a misfortune. He slipped on the ice climbing the front steps and broke his left hip. It was a bad fracture requiring surgery (he was in his fifties), and complications set in which resulted in a hospital stay of several weeks. After a long period of painful physiotherapy, he was pronounced fit and discharged.

On the way out of the hospital, Roy slipped on a wet tile in the lobby, and broke his *right* hip.

Back in his hospital bed, something snapped. A deep melancholy came over him as he endured his second convalescence in a gathering cloud of gloom. When at last his other hip recovered and he was again discharged, Roy limped carefully through the hospital lobby, drove home, went inside, and refused to come out again. We could see him staring out the kitchen window in his plaid dressing gown, day after day. Visitors at the front door were politely sent home. He would speak to nobody other than Aunt Ella. When we waved at him from the road, he would not wave back.

The village and the surrounding countryside, previously as comfortable and familiar as a private estate to Uncle Roy and to generations before him, had transformed into menacing, alien territory. Moreover, his fear of the world extended to the people in it—after all, if you can't trust the land you were born on, who or what *can* you trust?

Even the safety of his own snug kitchen failed to cheer him up. Brooding alone in his chair near the stove, staring out the window, his mood grew ever darker. He ceased to speak—even to Aunt Ella. Though reluctant to seek medical attention under any circumstances, let alone psychiatric distress, the family at length took Roy to the doctor in New Glasgow, who sent him to the hospital for observation—the hospital in the lobby of which he had broken his hip. After diagnosis ("clinical depression"), Uncle Roy was transferred to the provincial mental hospital, to be subjected to a series of electroshock treatments. It was not certain that he would ever come out again.

Around that time I telephoned home and asked my father: "How is Roy doing?"

"Roy's pretty down in the dumps," my father replied—the closest my father ever came to expressing the severity of Roy's condition.

Down in the dumps?

Uncle Roy had clearly wandered into a deep cave from which he would not emerge. He would spend his remaining days in a medicated fog. He would never again put out a fire, or sing in a choir, or take children on a sleigh ride, or tell a funny story. Roy had suffered the worst fate possible: He had lost his faith. It would not be putting it too strongly to say that in a fundamental way he had lost his life.

Down in the dumps?

A month later, after Heaven only knows what torment and indignity, Uncle Roy returned home from hospital. I asked my cousin how he was doing, and received this reply:

"Oh Roy's good! You wave at him, he'll wave right back!"

Well, that's a comfort.

Roy had returned to his solitary kitchen chair, unable to speak or to leave the house, but *he'll wave back now*. Possibly he waved back because he now knew what happens to you when you refuse: They take you away to Dartmouth Hospital and torture you.

Were my father and my cousin insane when they made these observations? Or had they uttered a kind of joke—a poker-faced, non-laughable joke, dry as sandpaper, too dry even for a smile? Canadians are sophisticated storytellers who savour black, ironic humour; have we perfected the poker-faced delivery to the point where *nobody* laughs?

Something very Canadian was happening here. In their determination to underplay Roy's tragedy and its implied threat to us all, the chosen language had become so insufficient to the scope of events as to indicate a desire to underplay life itself—like the habit of "knocking on wood" whenever expressing optimism or pleasure.

Canadians seem to nurse a superstition that, if we look straight at a thing, recognize it, and express it out loud, then we invite some sort of catastrophe. When something unfortunate happens, we pretend that it is not nearly as bad as it seems; when something auspicious happens, we invent some worry or caveat to play down our good luck. We feel Hemingway's need "not to put your mouth on it," never to utter a value judgement out loud (let alone to laugh or cry out loud), for fear that the very act of articulation will bring on some sort of trouble.

When I was a budding trumpet player, I was occasionally hired to play "The Last Post" at the funerals of Legionnaires. (The beginning of snow-shovelling season was an especially busy time.) Attending the funeral of a stranger lends one an objectivity normally lacking in such a situation, and I remember being struck by mourners' comparative cheer, their shared eagerness to maintain an upbeat mood, even if somebody happened to be dead.

Friends and family consciously avoided customary black garb in favour of a range of sporty jackets and dresses. Filing by the casket to view the corpse, it was not unusual to overhear someone comment on "how good he (or she) looks"—as though death had in some way improved the loved one's health. Later, as mourners gathered around the grave and I lifted my trumpet to serenade the final repose (accompanied by the hum of the casket elevator), I couldn't help noticing what a fine occasion death provided for friends to reunite, to share memories, and to catch up on the latest news.

Even today, as advancing age necessitates increased attendance at these events, I notice that, during the benediction, officiating clergy inevitably dismiss mourners with a caution not to "brood" over the death of the loved one: A few tears are well and good, but let us not make a fetish out of grief and get everyone "down in the dumps."

This necessity to diminish life's peaks and valleys has become so chronic over generations, we do it reflexively, without thinking how strange it might seem to others. To non-Canadians and to Quebecers it makes us "Anglos" appear anesthetized and wooden; yet it is an essential part of the Canadian option to both see and not see things at the same time, without which we would be unable to coexist.

To a writer it can necessitate leaving home, in order to see things in their true perspective, at their best and their worst. I began writing when I discovered that the only way to discern what I thought about a given topic was to consciously ask myself: "What is the *worst* thing I can say about this person or situation?" Only after I underwent this morbid exercise could I trust my observations to reflect something other than my childhood conditioning. To this day, whenever I look on the bright side, to my own ear I sound like someone who recently spent a large sum of money on human potential seminars.

Of course, life and death can only be diminished to a certain point, after which they begin to reassert themselves. Eventually, life's necessary patterns become so obvious, so inescapable, that looking on the bright side becomes impossible or possibly insane. When that happens, the Canadian response is to flip the whole thing over and turn it into a funny story.

The wry description of one's afflictions is at the centre of Canadian humour. Not only can we thereby avoid ending up like Uncle Roy, it enables us to compete on the North American comedy circuit: Canadians can joke about our own misfortune, whereas our American competitors, though perhaps more confident jokers, are confined to the misfortunes of others.

English Canada was forever altered by the waves of settlement, beginning in the early nineteenth century, of three generations of uprooted Celts.

During the highland clearances, whole septs of clans were driven from their ancestral land by the lairds and their English overlords for various reasons; mine were displaced in order to provide pasture for the wool industry.

According to my grandfather, my ancestors drifted from inland farms to the sea, which they hated and feared. Unskilled in fishing the "silver darlings" (a no doubt ironic term for herring), they eked out a sparse living gathering seaweed for sale as fertilizer. But they were no fools. Foreseeing a bleak prospectus in the seaweed business, they took the first opportunity to emigrate out of Aberdeen around 1820, puking their way over the Atlantic in the belly of the *Hector* on one of its many sailings to Pictou.

Having reached Nova Scotia, my ancestors proceeded straight inland by foot until the sea was well out of sight. They found a valley by a river, surrounded by a landscape that looked as much like Scotland as they could possibly hope for. There they created the village of Milltown, later to be renamed Hopewell for reasons nobody can remember. (Perhaps "Milltown" was not optimistic enough for them. Perhaps it made them feel "down in the dumps.")

A founding village population in the low hundreds built dwellings, a sawmill, dairy farms, a school, three churches—all the necessities for a relatively self-contained society whose members planned to take up where they had left off back home, and to stay put for generation after generation.

The culture that developed in Hopewell was predicated on one overriding intention: to stay. The utopian myth of frontier expansion held no charms for them, nor did the industrial wealth of cities. They had no desire to mine for gold or to eat in a restaurant. They were content.

And there they remain today, generations later, despite Hollywood movies and double-digit unemployment and two World Wars. To the enormous frustration of our social engineers in Ottawa, these people *do not want to move.*

The inhabitants of a village whose population plans to live and die there, and who plan for their children's children to do the same, behave very differently from a people who plan for their children to be moving on to better things. In a long-standing community such as this, the social stakes are far higher, if only because conflicts can go on for generations. Moreover, in a village like Hopewell the clan system of extended families dictates that if you make one enemy you make a hundred, and memories are long. My grandmother, a Cameron, could never bring herself to trust a Campbell after their treachery at Glencoe two centuries earlier; her cousin was a MacDonald, you see.

For a population this small to remain economically and socially viable, diverse enough to sustain itself with a minimal dependence on goods and services from outside, a tacit agreement had to be made to play down personal differences wherever possible. Farmers in overalls had to rub elbows with businessmen in suits; carpenters who had left school in Grade 6 had to make conversation with lawyers and schoolteachers on a daily basis. Tories and Grits had to depend upon each other for help in a crisis.

And they did. A passionate, at times violent people with a wide variety of skills, temperaments and intelligence quotients, they managed to get along with each other day after day, year after year, generation after generation, for over a century and a half.

Such harmony does not come cheap.

To make coexistence possible, villagers developed a set of unspoken rules governing social interaction, intuitively fashioned to head off conflicts before they occur—rules which were to apply themselves to the fabric of Canadian culture for generations to come, whose ethic of conformity and egalitarianism is best expressed by the all-Canadian question: *Who do you think you are?*

Eventually, of course, some villagers moved away—to create and augment towns like Truro and Stellarton a few miles away, to attend universities such as Acadia and Mount Allison (respect for education was greater than it is today), then to cities such as Halifax, Toronto and Vancouver. But even when they left the village they did not shed their acquired, unconscious patterns of social behavior. They applied them to their new situation so that, to this day, Canada's cities operate routinely according to the tacit rules established in tiny villages a century and a half ago.

This is why you will notice a person standing at a deserted intersection in Toronto, waiting for the "Walk" sign at four in the morning: not because he is afraid he will be caught, but because *those are the rules.* That is how things *are.* Just because it happens to be four in the morning, why should you be able to cross the street against the light? *Who do you think you are?*

The Scottish-Canadian village endured as the model for English Canada, through waves of immigration from other cultures. Like newcomers to any institution, succeeding immigrants quickly learned how to behave in Canada if you wanted to get along: For if you made one enemy you made a hundred. And memories ran long. And resentments ran deep.

Preemptive Insulation

Canadians have evolved a number of cultural devices designed to preempt conflict by creating an insulating no-man's-land of outward agreement and ritual goodwill. Two common examples, used in everyday life from sea to sea, are *the ritual apology* and *the weather.*

The ritual apology. The two most frequently-heard expressions in Canadian conversation are "Hello," and "I'm sorry." If a Canadian drops an object on the street and somebody else stoops to pick it up for him, the Canadian will murmur, not "Thank you," but "I'm sorry." If someone steps in front of a Canadian passing through a doorway, the Canadian who has suffered the inconvenience will apologize. If a minor verbal misunderstanding has taken place—as minor as the requirement of a sentence to be repeated in conversation—an apology will be expressed *by both parties.*

In Canada, ritual apologies occur in every situation containing so much as one second of uncertainty. Americans often interpret this habit as evidence of our diffidence and timidity, when it is nothing of the kind—as anyone who has been at the receiving end of a small town rumble will attest.

A New Glasgow lout perfectly capable of altering your face with his boot at a Legion Hall dance, upon brushing against a fellow lout in a doorway will mutter a reflexive "Sorry," as gallant as a lord. The lout himself will hardly know he is doing it, so conditioned is the ritual apology as a daily feature of long-term harmony, going back centuries.

This is not as inane as it may seem.

Any conflict between two human beings, no matter how quickly and easily resolved, has the potential to leave a faint residue of misunderstanding and ill will. In a small village these minor stains of residual resentment can build up, like the dirt in a bathtub that has not been cleaned.

Such accretions of gall eventually fester into nonspecific dislike—in which one person finds another offensive and does not quite know why. This vague, low-level hatred can spread to families and friends (How can they *stand* him? What kind of people *are* they?), building gradually over generations to the point where no resolution is possible, if only because there is nothing to resolve—there exists no identifiable area of dispute sufficiently grave to justify the depth of feeling.

The Scots who populated rural Canada in the early part of the nineteenth century, together with their portraits of lupine ancestors in tartans and animal skins, their recipes for blood pudding, and their precious inheritance of resentment going back to William Wallace, knew well the dark crevices of unspecific ill will that lie dormant in the human memory, crouched and ready to erupt when least expected.

By saying "I'm sorry," the prudent Canuck employs the Christian admonition to "turn the other cheek" *peremptorily*—a cunning device to head off minor conflicts and expunge residual resentments before they begin to show as a visible stain. "I'm sorry" instantly creates a layer of breathing space, of insulation at the point of interaction where two contrasting personalities contact and friction occurs.

American tourists marvel at the evident courtesy on the streets of Canadian cities—our amicable exchanges after car accidents and in other situations which, in Los Angeles or Detroit, could lead to shouts, physical contact and the display of arms. How is such harmony achieved? By offering a preemptive apology at every point of potential or imagined conflict throughout the day.

And by referring to *the weather.*

The Weather. No Canadian goes through the day without a few words about the weather. Street corner encounters, taxi and elevator rides, bank and drug store transactions—all contacts between acquaintances or strangers are rendered a little more palatable by an observation or two about the temperature, the amount of precipitation, together with a brief comparison with the previous day's meteorology and with yearly trends. (Echoing the misogynist nautical practice of naming hurricanes after women, the weather is always referred to as "She" or "It"—never "He.")

One reason for this preoccupation is that in Canada we *have* weather. Lots of it. Unlike, say, Jamaica ("Yes, it's sunny again, isn't it?"), Canadian weather is an ever-changing, powerful natural force that cannot be overcome, which, under certain circumstances, can kill you. In farming and fishing communities, the weather holds a rightful place as a more relevant, urgent and dynamic topic than, say, the progress of civil war in an unpronounceable foreign country.

There is something laudable in Canadians' respect for the weather: a bracing realism that may save us yet.

Every winter a major blizzard hits the "snow belt"—a meteorological pattern running from Southern Ontario, through northern New York State and Michigan, south as far as Illinois. Whenever such a blizzard occurs (and they are as regular as winter), the Detroit and Buffalo newspapers report at least a half-dozen fatalities: Some poor soul decides to walk to the corner store in shirtsleeves for cigarettes and is found by the postman next morning, seated quietly beside a fire hydrant, stiff as a cod.

But you seldom hear of such a thing happening in London, Windsor, or in any of the dozens of Ontario municipalities a few miles north of the border—whose citizens, even to take out the garbage, bundle up in down-filled parkas that make them look like hand grenades.

(With sad irony, such deaths have recently been known to happen in Yellowknife, when the victim is very young, very drunk, and has been watching too much TV from California.)

It all has to do with the word *north*. To Americans, the word evokes a primarily social and urban landscape—the industrial heartland, home of Lincolnesque liberalism, Brooks Brothers suits and Harvard University. To Canadians on the other hand, *north* evokes a vast existential death symbol, a mystical space in which mankind has no power and no place.

To Canadians, *north* is where the weather comes from.

We respect the weather because we know it can kill you. It cannot be beaten. We have no frontier myth of man conquering nature to delude us into strolling outdoors in a T-shirt at forty below. There is humility here, a respect for the universal machinery perhaps lacking in the United States—with its southern, anthropocentric assumptions.

But a more important reason for the weather to preoccupy us, even in the climate-controlled malls of contemporary Edmonton and Toronto, traces back to the preemptive apology. Here we have an area of certain agreement, a cushion of confluence allowing one Canadian to slip past another without even the remote possibility of argument or enmity. Together with *I'm sorry*, the weather allows the villager and his urban ancestor to stroll through the day confident that he has not, through some misguided remark, blundered into a blood feud.

Of course every device for social interaction exacts a fee. The elimination of potential conflict preempts the possibility of *contact* as well—which occurs at the boundary where one personality meets another, where the border between two minds is recognized and acknowledged.

All differences carry an element of inherent risk. If we spend our lives in agreement, apologizing and talking about the weather, we may avoid conflict, but we will never get to know one another. The village lives in harmony, but it is an accord of strangers passing silently in the fog.

On the other hand, there are worse ways to channel conflict and ill will. There is the European penchant for diverting resentments in the direction of scapegoats such as the Gypsies or the Jews or the local witch, who become receptacles for undercurrents of malice—infections to be lanced with periodic eruptions of officially condoned or ignored violence. On occasion, the Canadian village has employed this device as well; in place of Jews and Gypsies, our scapegoat of choice has been Asians, Haitians, Jamaicans, Afro-Americans and Native people.

But given a choice, Canadians prefer to apologize than to kill or maim. Although we enjoy the same diet of violence in our broadcast media as anyone else in North America, when we turn off the TV, we would rather talk about the weather.

A Bunker of Cheer

Whatever our denomination, the cornerstone of Canadian morality holds that the way to become a good person is to *act* like one. The pursuit of wisdom, with its faint whiff of intellectual narcissism and elite skepticism, can find itself at odds with faith and thus lead one, however intelligently, straight to Hell.

At the heart of the Canadian Christian tenet known as the "social gospel" is the desire to externalize faith. To *be* good is to *do* good, that is, to imitate a good person. In theory, the good person to be imitated is Jesus Christ—but exactly how is that done? Where is the opportunity in contemporary life to heal the sick, to turn the other cheek, to suffer persecution and martyrdom? As a child walking home from Sunday school I was painfully aware of my inability to effect the Gospel in real life. It was, after all, conceived, preached and transcribed several thousand years ago, in a hot, dry country with a more competitive lifestyle.

Unable to imitate the remote and impossible Christ, Canadians focus on good people we know, or think we know—Dad and Mom, or possibly the local fireman. Should the family or community fail to provide suitably elevated role models—which is usually the case—then we imitate somebody we see on TV. (My personal icon was Paladin, the black-clad, chess-playing, soft-hearted mercenary in *Have Gun, Will Travel.* Sometimes I think I am still trying to imitate Paladin.)

Our desire not to contemplate the spiritual and moral questions of the day, but rather to follow in some good person's footsteps and to express our borrowed virtue in good works, has given Canada the safety nets which define our social character when compared to the United States. An evident will to do good contributes to our international reputation as "honest brokers"—a well-meaning, progressive force. (If you want to see a confused American, inform him that the founders of the Canadian socialist movement were not atheists and Jews, but *Baptists.*)

Rather than thinking about life, we would prefer to grit our teeth and do good, resulting in that characteristic Canadian expression—lips up, teeth clenched—that is often mistaken for a smile. But seeking to do good can have its drawbacks—especially when it is done to avoid thinking about something bad. When we do good for the feeling and not the result, we are only *pretending* to do good. We can delude ourselves into thinking we're bound for Heaven, when in fact we are going to Hell.

For many Canadians, universal social programs are good even if they do no good, because they are admissible evidence that *we mean to do good.* If we revise our universal social programs, it is argued, then we will have a "two-tiered" system—as though Canada were not a staircase of unearned privilege already—and we will not be good anymore. Thus, we wed ourselves to an outmoded system that is failing, out of a wish to avoid thinking about the frightening issue of human inequality.

The role of fate and chance in life is an implied threat to every Canadian—that bad things can happen and good things can be taken away at any moment, for no reason. What did we do to deserve the largest piece of geography on the planet, with the highest overall standard of living in the history of the human race? Why should it not be arbitrarily taken away from us? Easy come, easy go.

Baffled and unnerved by our good fortune, we tiptoe back and forth as though an anvil were poised above our heads, hanging by a thread—as though when the world queued up for national punishment, Canadians were temporarily overlooked. We are not really timid; we are merely trying not to draw critical attention to ourselves. Making ourselves scarce. Hoping for the best. Trying to do good. Talking about the weather.

A Traditional Disgrace

Yet good and evil do exist in real life—and if you pretend otherwise, evil can exist right under your nose for a very long time.

We read about the Christian Brothers of Mount Cachel and the choir master in Kingston, indulging in the ongoing sexual abuse of young students for decades; or about a teacher in Alberta routinely instructing history students that the Nazi extermination of Jews never occurred; and the uncomfortable question comes to mind: *Didn't people know?* How could such antisocial behavior escape notice, in communities where discreet marital infidelities become common knowledge before the sheets are cold?

Was no administrator, cleric or janitor party to a whisper that something untoward might be happening at Mount Cachel—for decades? Was there no inkling among parents and teachers in Eckville that some of the material Jim Keegstra was teaching was not on the provincial curriculum—year after year?

Of course there was.

Here we see examples, thousands of miles apart, of the darker side of the imaginary country, in which evil grows malignant thanks to that basic social device of the Canadian village—*the ability to see and not to see at the same time.*

The Canadian village did not develop out of a cultural revolution, nor was it established by utopian rebels acting out their vision of the human potential. We were not inspired by Rousseau and Tom Paine to make a clean break with a European heritage going back to the Holy Roman Empire. We brought the old world to Canada—all of it. We were not about to propose a new one. We took our roots, all of them, and transplanted them in Canadian soil, where they continue to flourish under the name of multiculturalism.

The trouble is, some of these roots were rotten—had mutated over the years into something grotesque.

At the Commission on Child Labour in 1815, British parliamentarians heard the testimony of Elizabeth Bentley, a worker in a flax mill since the age of six. At this typical factory, eight-year-olds walked two miles to and from work, where they toiled from five in the morning until nine at night, with one forty-minute meal break and no water in between. Anguished parents complained that they could not keep their children awake long enough to eat. When they fell asleep at work, children were docked a day's pay. They were routinely flogged, often to the point of unconsciousness.

These conditions were not atypical. Royal commissioners received such testimony with distaste, but not with anything like the shriek of outrage that accompanies the subject of child abuse today.

The protection of children in a sheltered category as "minors" is a relatively recent phenomenon in European history. Until the advent of nineteenth-century Romanticism, children were regarded as apprentice adults: uncivilized, imbued with chaotic tendencies that rendered them potentially evil. (This was the excuse for patronizing Indians as "children," and for the conditions in native schools.)

The European child's education took the form of animal training, with the avoidance of torture as a prime incentive. Likewise, child criminals were hanged just like adults—even if executioners were required to pull on the legs of ten-year-olds to achieve the desired result.

No point pretending otherwise: These are traditional values, part of our heritage, part of the imaginary Canada.

Traditionally, only the mother of a European child could be expected to feel any real warmth for the creature, and without parents a child was well and truly lost. Orphans were demoted to a slightly sub-human category reserved for criminals, defectives and fallen women. Such creatures became a convenient outlet for anti-social but very human impulses—the desire to torment, to rape, to *abuse*—that might otherwise have disturbed the continuity of the village.

In this context, let us look at the Christian Brothers and the sordid revelations at Mount Cachel—not as a modern phenomenon but as an ancient tradition, transplanted to the new world in its entirety, nurtured by the benign avoidance so essential to Canadian culture: the ability to see and not see at the same time.

Following the collapse of the Holy Roman Empire, Christianity became the bastion of classical civilization against the arbitrary violence of barbarian warlords. The Church became a transcendent nation-state, an imaginary country with no precise borders—and no legal tax base—whose mission was to amass maximum power and wealth in the defence of civilization. This required a certain amount of moral compromise for the greater good. Politics and intrigue crept into church affairs, and at times the Pope was not the holiest of men. Clerics became highly adept at seeing and not seeing at the same time.

Enforced celibacy among the Roman Catholic priesthood had nothing to do with the Bible, and everything to do with the Church's institutional genius for amassing wealth by ensuring that, once acquired, little of it escapes. Celibacy ensured that the priest died without legitimate heirs, and his inheritance was funnelled into the Church. Other considerations cited in defence of abstinence—sacred duty, the demand of absolute commitment—formed the spiritual pretext for what was essentially a matter of estate management.

Virtually everyone experiences the sexual urge at one time or another with varying intensity. How was the church to accommodate celibate Christian brothers with, shall we say, more specialized and urgent needs—needs that were not sublimated by prayer but continued to fester throughout the day, distracting these men from their holy work?

Like the torturing of criminals, the burning of witches and the persecution of Jews, the sexual *use* of orphans (after all, *abuse* applies to full-fledged human beings) ensured the smooth functioning of the Church in the community. All the Church and the community needed to do, to benefit from this harmonious arrangement, was to agree not to see it.

Quite an accomplishment. Such a compact goes well beyond a refusal to acknowledge objective fact, for it requires one to refuse to acknowledge it *even to oneself*. Yet it is a mental technique Canadians acquire early in life, one we employ on a daily basis.

We see and fail to see semi-institutionalized incest in isolated communities—although everybody knows. Somehow it fails to occur to us that our neighbour is an alcoholic—although he frequently slurs his speech and has a number of minor traffic accidents. Similarly, we both see and do not see the bruise under his wife's eye—no doubt she ran into a door. And we overlook our local political representative's improved standard of living since taking office.

When a Kingston choir director was charged and convicted with sexually abusing young boys for years (resulting in at least one suicide), a remarkable amount of resentment on the part of the congregation was aimed, not at the choir director, but at the church officials who laid charges. The choir director was such a nice man, you see. So talented. His choirs had won a number of international awards.

So fiercely do Canadians defend our right to see and not see, you would think consciousness itself was a matter of personal choice. The controversial United Church decision to allow homosexuals to enter the ministry was not really about allowing homosexuals to preach in church, but about *seeing* homosexuals preaching in church. Canadian villagers have for generations lived side by side with long-term bachelors and spinsters—living together as "roommates of long standing"—without incident. At issue here is not the verb "to admit" in the sense of "to permit to enter," but "to admit" in the sense of "to acknowledge fact." To admit homosexuals to the United Church ministry would mean acknowledging that there have been homosexuals in the village all along, that we saw and did not see at the same time.

What else have we been seeing and not seeing at the same time? What revelations are to come?

A Nice Guy

Now to get to Eckville you take the side road off the Trans-Canada, and head right to the end as far as you can go. There's a main street, a post office, and a 7-11. Not many people pass through Eckville. People who come here generally come to stay.

Jim was a popular man here, in fact he still is. A former mayor of the village, a veteran high school teacher, he taught school for years, all the young people passed through one of Jim's history classes at one time or another. Runs the gas station now, down at the end of the street—since he was forced out of teaching after his trouble.

Jim's friendly. He'll give you a hand. You see him at the curling rink regularly in the winter, plays ball in the summer. Pretty good curler. Jim was and in a way still is what you might call a pillar of the community. He's what you would call a nice guy.

What got him in trouble was that he was teaching his history classes that the Jewish Holocaust never happened—or at least wasn't as bad as they say. Used some material sent from the States, the sort of stuff that tells you white people are an endangered species, that the Chinese and the East Indians are out to get us. Maybe so. Sure are a lot more of them around than there used to be.

Jim thinks it's the Jews. They've got the money, they control the government, the press, everything. I don't think he's necessarily right on that, but who's to say? Who in the heck's making money off the deficit, collecting all that interest, can you tell me that?

Now we all knew Jim had some strong opinions, and I suppose it occurred to us that he was moving a bit outside the curriculum now and then, but so what? It isn't as though he wasn't teaching them the course material. Jim was a good teacher. His kids knew their dates, their battles, always did well in their Provincials.

Now I know anti-Semitism isn't necessarily a good thing—my dad was wounded overseas fighting Hitler, for Heaven's sake—but keep in mind: *There are no Jews in Eckville!* Not one Jewish person in the village. So just tell me, who's the victim here? Where's the harm? It isn't as if the place was about to go on a *pogrom* or anything. There's hardly any crime here. You can leave your front door unlocked for a week, nobody will steal from you.

OK, fine. Some kids graduated from high school thinking the Holocaust was a little bit exaggerated, it's regrettable, but what in heck's the difference? If Jim's wrong, let them prove it. There was no need to send in the RCMP over it. Unless there's something to what he says.

Jim's one of the most well-liked guys in this village. It isn't as if he's a criminal. You'd trust your house to Jim, you'd lend him your car—and if you did I guarantee it would come back with a full tank of gas.

Jim's not a thinker, he likes to *do* things for people. Member of the volunteer fire department, regular churchgoer, Scout leader, coach: He may have some different ideas but it never affected his daily life. He's the nicest guy you'd ever want to meet.

OK, fine. Let's say the Holocaust really did happen. Nothing Jim says or does is going to change that. Besides, if he genuinely believes in his heart that the whole thing was part of a plan to make white people give them Israel, who can say for sure it isn't true? Can *you* prove it isn't true? Look at the Bronfmans, the Reichmans—the papers are full of them. You never know who's pulling the strings.

It was that family from Ontario started kicking up a fuss over something their kid brought home from school. Politically correct types, they took it to the principal, the press, the province, the CBC, it was ridiculous! They didn't have to turn it into a circus. If they'd have sat down with Jim and expressed their concerns there would have been no need to drag Eckville's reputation through the gutter because of a couple of things in a scribbler. Jim wouldn't hurt a soul. They didn't have to do a thing like that.

I never heard him say anything bad about Jews. Nicest fellow on the face of the earth, teaching what he sincerely believed to be true. Is that supposed to be against the law now? The way the courts are chasing after Jim when there are so many *real* criminals out there, it almost makes you think there's something to what he says.

It will take a long time for Eckville to get over this.

THE VISIT:
A DOMESTIC WILDERNESS EXPERIENCE

Family Pets

Sooner or later, every Canadian comes into contact with the fundamentally primitive, alien character of the national landscape, the primordial slime underneath the rock in the garden. A hiker in northern Ontario is driven mad by blackflies and dies of exposure; a ten-year-old Vancouver Island boy is eaten by a cougar; or an amateur photographer is snatched from a rock by the waves at Peggy's Cove and washed out to sea.

These small, discomfiting glimpses of the landscape's true character question the Victorian vision our forebears carried with them from Europe, along with their volumes of Wordsworth, A.A. Milne and the Bible; their need to bring the natural environment into line with what they wanted to believe, to minimize the lurking suspicion that there might be something out there, a living presence just out of sight, that is neither our servant nor our friend.

In a minor way, such an experience occurred to my family the day the brother came home with the snapping turtle.

The brother meant well. Mother had been quiet since the disappearance of the robin she had raised from such an early age that it had been necessary to crush the worms manually before feeding it.

This solution she reached by trial and error. First she shoved the soft, blind creatures down the bird's beak with her forefinger—only to have them scramble right back out in a desperate rout for life. Then she tried easing the worms in one by one, like lengths of miniature hose; the young bird successfully packed the worm into his craw, but almost immediately we could discern frantic movement, like a kicking under the bedclothes, and soon the hysterical worm would reappear, squirming to freedom. Clearly young robins could not eat whole worms, and a simple operation proved that they could not eat halved worms either. The worms would have to be crushed to a pulp before serving (as though they had not been through enough already). Mother, who was not squeamish about a thing, did this. Every day she crushed and fed worms to the tiny bird, on a schedule suggested by *The Encyclopædia Britannica.*

It was said that Mother inherited her scientific bent from my grandfather. She viewed nature unsentimentally, with the detached interest a biologist accords a dissected frog. Father took an entirely different view: a religious man who believed that God sees the little sparrow fall, he tended to regard the natural world as a series of staggering anthropomorphisms.

Thus, while Mother crushed worms and stuffed them down the robin's neck, Father named him Fred.

Miraculously, Fred survived both world views, but that fall the inevitable occurred. Mother called Fred to the back stoop—and nobody came. Without so much as a cheep for a thank you, he had gone to seek his fortune, which was probably a brief and chilly one since he had been brought up to trust people.

Into this benign set of Beatrix Potter assumptions crawled Martha.

Hitch-hiking home from Halifax late at night, the brother was picked up by a Volkswagen Beetle. Somewhere around Enfield the driver spotted a dark lump moving slowly across the midnight highway, and remarked that he had never seen such a turtle in all his life.

The brother, who may or may not have been drinking, immediately seized on the notion that this turtle was just the thing to bring home to Mother, to replace Fred.

Even in the uncertain light of the headlamps it was clear that this was a damned odd-looking turtle, truly unsettling to look at. Something about the animal evoked deep, genetic memories of a time when the night and the forest teemed with flesh-eating predators on the prowl.

74

Its shell was about two feet long—not shiny and smooth like friendly domestic turtles, but mucky and black, with an irregular dinosaur-like ridge along its craggy surface, a mass of lumps and ridges with no trace of symmetry or shape. Its head was normally tucked into its shell and out of sight, but on occasions of alarm a bald skull the size of your fist would emerge on the end of a neck at least ten inches long, serpent-like, lipless, eyebrowless and truly revolting to the human eye. Furthermore, its rasp-like tail dragged behind, long and spiny, adding another six inches to the overall length of the beast, bringing it to a good three feet when fully stretched out.

Somehow the brother convinced the driver that it would be a good thing to put the beast into the trunk and take it home.

The driver began to have second thoughts when they tried to pick it up and the neck reached its full extension, whipping back and forth ferociously with the head hissing, cobra-like, snapping at their arms and faces, mouth clicking like an amateur castanet player, and it became apparent that this was one vicious jumbo of a snapping turtle, fully capable of removing half your hand in one snap.

The brother assured him that everything was under control (it was not), and that he knew what he was doing (he did not). Using a water-logged sheet of plywood from the ditch, they manoeuvred the hissing, clicking reptile into the Volkswagen's tiny front-end trunk.

Back on their way, the brother chatted amiably in order to distract the driver's attention from the muffled snapping coming from the front of the car. They still had twenty miles to go when the headlamps began to flash on and off of their own accord, emitting some desperate, enigmatic code. Evidently, the turtle was eating through the electrical wiring; in fact it was reaming out the trunk.

By the time they deposited the creature on our asphalt driveway, using a snow shovel from the garage, even the spare tire had been slashed to pieces.

The brother said good night to the driver, locked the creature in the garage, and went to bed with the sense of satisfaction that comes from a difficult job well done.

The driver drove home. He would never again pick up another hitchhiker as long as he lived.

A Mixed Reception

When she saw the turtle the next day, Mother was intrigued.

"My goodness, isn't that fascinating," she said. "I wonder what you feed it."

She leafed through *The Encyclopædia Britannica* and obtained various facts about the turtle, such as how to determine its sex, which was female.

While Mother studied the encyclopedia, Father named her Martha.

Yet despite her name, he did not warm to the animal right away. An insurance inspector with a keen eye for the potential hazard, he saw a hazard squatting there in the garage if there ever was one—and he was right. Martha was from another place and time, did not want to be here, and did not like us. She would never be persuaded to heel or to fetch, in fact she responded to every overture with renewed spasms of hissing and snapping, whipping about at random with that bony ridge of a mouth, determined to make somebody regret her abduction for the rest of his life.

On the other hand, although Martha was not quite his style as a pet, neither was it in Father's nature to speak ill of one of God's creatures.

"Martha has spirit," he remarked, after a narrow escape in which he nearly lost a thumb.

The brother was summoned to explain Martha's presence, but of course he could not be found, being of the age when a person effectively disappears from family life and is rarely spotted, except at the refrigerator and on the way to or from the toilet. When confronted that evening, he could not remember the exact spot where he had picked up Martha and, since Father would never abandon the beast anywhere but in her own neighbourhood ("How would *you* like to be thrown into a strange swamp miles from home?"), we were at an impasse that continued for the rest of the week.

Mother determined what kind of food she would eat, which turned out to be just about anything, including cats and people given the chance. We fed her anything nonvegetarian that happened to be lying around—hamburger, cat food, and a goldfish the brother had killed by over-feeding.

Like any guest in our house Martha soon gained acceptance, and by Friday Father no longer regarded her as an animal at all, but more like a reclusive but respected tenant, or a distant, eccentric relative who had once done him a good turn. "Martha doesn't have much to say," he would chuckle once or twice a day in one of his ongoing, low-level jokes.

"How is Martha doing?" he would ask, as we sat down to dinner or supper.

"Just fine," Mother would reply. "She ate a rat Harold found downtown."

Father would nod, approvingly. "Good for her."

That Monday, however, Martha disappeared.

"Martha's gone," Mother announced over breakfast, perplexed.

In what was for him an unusually violent gesture, Father put down his copy of the *Chronicle-Herald* and took off his glasses: "Oh, bless my soul," he said.

Years of experience with damage claims flashed through his mind, images of children with lost thumbs, public disgrace, expensive liability premiums and a lifetime of rue. As her hosts, we would be required to pay the tab for Martha's behavior throughout her stay in Truro, whereas Martha was beholden to us for nothing at all.

Father had the local RCMP detachment on the line before he finished his eggs. He felt deeply embarrassed by this emergency. Respectable people, in his view, did not have emergencies. Emergencies happened to people who had failed to think things through. If everyone exercised proper foresight and caution, the world would be a safer place to live.

The RCMP, Canada's instrument of public caution, put out an all points bulletin for a large snapping turtle. A second call to the local radio station resulted in a public warning, just before the school march and the farm report.

The brother, having come down in his pyjamas to open the refrigerator, asked Father innocently what all the fuss was about.

On his way out the door, Father gave the brother a look.

Fortunately, Martha was found within the hour, not hacking off the young limbs of schoolchildren, but making her way down Willow Street toward the Halifax highway at her glacial pace, with the serenity of a long-term government employee at pension time, singing: "Goin' home, goin' home, Lawd I's goin' home."

Two tall, puzzled young RCMP constables returned her to the driveway in a wheelbarrow, then gave Mother a warning that we had better get this turtle out of town because if this sort of thing happened again the reptile would have to be destroyed.

"Would you like a cup of tea?" Mother replied.

A Frightening Experience

Surprisingly, the episode did not disgrace Martha in Father's sight—in fact, the roots of a friendship had germinated. As far as he was concerned Martha was only doing what any home-loving Canadian of Scottish descent would under similar circumstances, which made her practically a relative. As he mentioned to the brother in significant tones, if everyone had the same regard for the home, the world would not be in the shape it is in today.

"That Martha is quite a girl," he would say under his breath, in a voice loaded with Celtic understatement.

At length it was decided that Martha would be relocated at our summer cottage in Pictou some forty miles away, where she could be fenced in safely, and where she would be "more at home." The family could pay her weekend visits until the summer holidays, "to see if there was anything she needed."

Father and I manoeuvred Martha into a large galvanized washtub (Snap! Hiss! Click!), and placed the tub into the back seat of our Chevrolet Biscayne. Of course, the brother was nowhere to be found. I was given the responsibility of driving her to Pictou, where I was to see that she was "settled in."

Under other circumstances, I should have welcomed the opportunity to drive the family car, having just passed my driver's test after three tries; but not in this case. For I was afraid of Martha. There had never been established in my mind any certain limits to the creature, which inspired in me the sort of inter-species paranoia one feels when confronted with a good-sized rat—the irrational fear that the rodent can somehow sink his little teeth into one's eye. Similarly, in my mind Martha was perfectly capable of scaling the walls of the galvanized washtub and taking a good chunk out of the back of my neck before we reached North River.

It might have been different had Martha been in the passenger seat where I could see her as I drove, but she was in the *back* seat, and chills of dread shot up and down my spine as we drove down Queen Street, through Bible Hill and onto the Pictou Highway.

I cursed the brother as I sped through Kemptown, certain that at any second a lipless, reptilian head at the end of a two-foot-long neck would crane its way over my shoulder into my peripheral vision—and what then? Would I swerve the Chevrolet onto the shoulder, shrieking hysterically, startling Martha into dreadful activity? Or would I continue to drive in a sweating terror, praying to God that she would not start that frightful whiplike movement of her neck, punctuated by the castanets, each penetrating click heralding the loss of a good quarter-pound of flesh? Remember, the human head has not all that much flesh to spare. Of the thigh you can do without a bit, but you cannot hack above the shoulders for long without causing permanent damage.

Insane calculations raced through my mind as I drove—the sort of deals a person makes with himself while being attacked by a grizzly in Banff: "If I play dead and give him a chew of the calf, maybe he will be momentarily sated and, after pissing on me, will leave me to crawl home with what remains."

My hands gripped the steering wheel, numb with tension. Each hiss seemed a bit closer to my ear than the one before. I could hear her rummaging around back there; in my mind's eye she had already escaped the washtub and was crawling along the back seat. It was all I could do not to simply open the door and leap out of the moving car.

Finally we reached the turnoff onto the winding dirt road to shore and the Chevrolet bumped its way down the hill to the clearing where the cottage sat, white with red trim, windows boarded up for the winter, facing the cold Atlantic ocean. I switched off the engine and turned around, slowly.

Martha sat in the washtub, still and silent, staring balefully up at me, her bony head protruding slightly from her inelegant shell.

Using some scraps from the tool shed, I constructed a crude corral of chicken wire around a small pond on a marshy bit of land in the nearby woods, populous enough with frogs and vermin to allow Martha to feed herself. When I overturned the washtub inside this hastily constructed pen, she seemed to sense that I meant no harm. By the time I had returned the tools to the shed she was sliding into the pond, looking like something out of a heavy metal comic book.

Quite a Girl

The following summer was typical—hot, brown and salty, played to the drone of outboard motors and rock and roll from Philadelphia. Mother carried out various experiments with plant and sea life, and tried weaving reed baskets the way the Micmac did, with mixed success. Father mowed, painted and hammered away, in his lifelong quest for the improvement of property.

Behind the chicken wire in the woods, even Martha seemed to succumb to that atmosphere of unhurried, methodical calm that overcame everyone (except the brother, habitually out all night, whose skin remained urban white). It became possible to pick Martha up by her shell without being attacked, although I would never try it, and one Sunday morning I wandered out the back door with my oatmeal porridge and was horrified to see Father gently petting her phlegmatic head, with two fingers as vulnerable as uncooked sausages.

"Nice Martha. And how is Martha today? There, there."

Mother meanwhile made various notes about Martha in a Hilroy notebook. In early August she had an announcement to make: "Martha appears to be pregnant."

This development presented a whole new series of problems: We might now become the keepers of not one but many snapping turtles—top of the food chain predators who would make the back-yard only slightly less treacherous than a pond full of crocodiles.

"What are we going to do about Martha?" Father asked rhetorically, for it was clear that a decision had already been made. "The life we have to offer her is no life for a turtle."

Martha would be given a new home in a large swamp about half a mile into the backwoods. Mother agreed that this was the best plan, since Martha would want to burrow into the mud and hibernate for winter.

That afternoon Father, Mother and myself (the brother could not be found) carried Martha out to the large swamp for the first and last time. She did not resist and, as Father put it, "didn't have much to say." Mother painted "Martha" onto the edge of her shell (she liked to tag animals, birds and fish for some reason), and placed her at the edge of the pond. After a moment's hesitation, Martha flopped into the turbid water and disappeared.

We returned to school. Father went back to the office. Mother conducted experiments involving vitamins.

On weekend trips to the cottage, Father would regularly tramp through the woods to the swamp and call Martha's name, "just in case there was something she needed." But he never saw her again. She had gone her own way, which had nothing whatever to do with us.

In my mind's eye, I can still see Father staring at the water as evening fell, swatting mosquitoes and thinking about something.

A Tale of Two Villages:
Saviours with Forked Tongues

Oh Baby Allons
(Laissez-moi vous prenez vers l'action)

Throughout the 1960s, the best way to get from Truro to Montreal was by train.

Airplanes were faintly decadent, associated with foreign holidays, and the Halifax airport was located miles from the city—you faced added outlay just getting to and from the airport, plus the cost of the airline ticket. The automobile, convenient when running, became economical only when a bone-crush of passengers shared gasoline expenses, sandwiched like refugees through a miserable, sweaty night. (A motel would distort the budget beyond recognition.)

Hitchhiking was an attractive option, for the serial killer had yet to become a media personality. At worst, the hitchhiker endured an unwanted sexual advance, or a drunk, or a bore, or a family of smokers with a virus.

The problem with hitchhiking was that you never knew when you might arrive, for drivers feared hitchhikers then as they do now—although for some reason they were more willing to pick you up if you carried a sign with the name of your destination on it. (Perhaps the fact that you could spell was of some comfort. I knew a hitchhiker who enjoyed some success with the word "harmless.")

And, since a motel was an even less economical option for a hitchhiker than for a driver, you spent at least one night shivering in the acid green concentration camp glare of a Trans-Canada intersection, delirious with boredom and fatigue; or you slept in a jail—usually in Edmonston, New Brunswick or in Rivière de Loup, Quebec—where a bored sheriff took your wallet, belt and shoelaces and escorted you to your unhygienic bed.

I was put off this practice after a bad experience in a New Brunswick town in which the jail was a cage at the rear of the bus station garage. At six in the morning all three buses started up at once; by the time they unlocked my cell I was nearly gassed.

On the positive side, hitchhiking to Montreal made a culturally educational journey, in that the transition from English to French took place in measured steps. As you passed through New Brunswick, commercial signs gradually acquired accents and cathedral spires multiplied, until by the time you reached the Gaspé Peninsula even the pop music had changed. Instead of The Beach Boys and Freddy Cannon, the revolving roster on the chrome restaurant jukebox carried a choice of unfamiliar names, such as Les Classels and Pierre LaLonde. To an Anglo teenager with a Beatle haircut, this was exotic stuff.

The expenditure of a quarter, however, revealed that things were not as unfamiliar as they appeared, for the songs recorded by Les Têtes Blanches and Les Eccentriques were in fact nothing more than cover versions of Beach Boys and Freddy Cannon hits, with translated lyrics—"Oh baby allons, laissez-moi vous prenez vers l'action," and "Il y'a fume fume fume jusque'a Daddy prends le T-Bird"—pushing the beat in that distinctive Quebecois fashion that sounds rushed to the English ear.

Still, Les Classels made hitchhiking to Montreal a refreshing experience in a homogenizing world—the first couple of times, at least.

But for any Nova Scotian traveling on limited time and money, the ideal way to Montreal was to take the Ocean Limited: safe, relatively punctual, and twenty-two dollars if you sat up, and avoided the fraudulent cheese sandwiches—narrow strips piled generously at the visible edges, masking a single Kraft cheese slice at the centre, as thin as a leaf. A dollar twenty!

84

Early the next morning, with a crick in your neck and a foul taste in your mouth, you pressed your face to the cold window as the coach creaked its way into Queen Elizabeth Station near Place Ville-Marie in the heart of Montreal.

Then you stepped onto University Avenue, and suddenly you could breathe.

Outside

The Esquire Showbar on Stanley Street sported rococo pillars and a mirrored ceiling; the bar surrounded a thrust stage where Memphis soul bands such as Junior Walker and the All-Stars played and danced, flat out. At Rockhead's Palace, another Harlem club, the bass player with the house band wore an iridescent green suit of sufficient size that his Fender Bassman looked like a tennis racquet strapped to his stomach, as he stood there, majestically still, only the fingers and the eyes moving throughout the most frenetic numbers. (I am still fascinated by that bass player in the green suit and wonder where he is now—dead, probably. I was too young to wonder why the strippers wore bruises.)

A twenty-minute walk northwest took me from Rockhead's Palace to Mountain Street, which for a young man from Nova Scotia was like walking from New York to Paris. Pharaoh Sanders and Grachan Moncur III played at the Black Bottom; across the street at Le Bistro, over marble tables covered with Dow and Laurentide beer, McGill students discussed weighty matters, while at a corner table Leonard Cohen murmured into the ear of a young Jewish woman: "Have you suffered?"

To the east along Sherbrooke Street was the New Penelope, where I listened to precocious university rock by groups such as The Mothers of Invention and The Sidetrack. Up a narrow staircase across the street was L'Association Espagnol, where beer was served until dawn, *Chansonières* in black T-shirts strummed guitars, and a young Nova Scotian reached the outer limits of Bohemia.

Eventually I slept—at the apartments of friends, or friends of friends, or complete strangers, like the woman who wrote for *Midnight* and *The Enquirer*, pieces with titles such as "I was Raped by a Man from Outer Space." Judy had taken a fancy to belladonna, which she obtained by boiling the contents of asthmatic cigarettes into a vile tea, which she then drank. It made you hallucinate vivid yet mundane activities: You would get up, go into the kitchen, make yourself a sandwich...then realize that you had not done any of those things.

In Montreal I met blacks, Jews, and French-Canadians—"minority groups" for whom any white Anglo, Nova Scotian or not, was a target for reflex hostility and suspicion. For the first time I encountered people who distrusted me, disliked me even, for reasons not personal but historical.

I could not care less. A slight chill in the atmosphere is small discomfort when you have just emerged from the village where everyone knows your uncle, where every move you make is under discussion and where, if you fail to make a conscious effort to develop your curiosity, your brain will shrink to the size of a pea.

Up for Air

What created this intoxicating atmosphere of liberation was the presence of a language other than English. All around you, in the streets and the bistros and the clubs, people spoke *French*.

When you hear people living day to day in another language, the words you are accustomed to putting to things no longer seem so...absolute. By extension, everything that has ever been said to you in your own language is open to question. The world becomes comparative, since nobody has the last word on how to describe it. The assumed truth about yourself, the names you have been called and have absorbed—none of it is necessarily true. All bets are now off.

This came as a divine revelation to the fat boy from Truro who played the piano and could not fight.

Not that I could speak a word of it. The French taught in a Nova Scotia school would not be recognizable anyplace else. And Francophones are touchy about the sound of their language: To speak English with a French accent may sound European and debonair, but for French-Canadians to hear the language butchered by the drawl of an Anglo is to listen to fingernails scratching on a blackboard. For that reason, it is maddeningly difficult to practise your French in Quebec. People switch to English as though by clairvoyance the moment you enter the room.

But to me, none of this mattered one bit. In Montreal at that time, French was not the subject of attention it is today, French was the *environment*: the air that allowed the cultural life—the Esquire, the Bistro, the crowds singing on St. Denis St.—to breathe. Language created a climate that enabled me to escape the village in my mind.

Of course I heard the complaint that you could not buy a pair of trousers at Eaton's, in French. That pair of pants at Eaton's came up time and again as the quintessential indignity for the Francophone Quebecois. I could not imagine why a French-Canadian would *want* to buy their pants at Eaton's. Wherever they did buy their trousers, they dressed far more stylishly than us Anglos, and ate better as well: What more did they want?

If you took an interest in federal politics during the Lester Pearson years (few did), "What does Quebec want?" was the question of the day. Whatever it was, some of them wanted it badly enough to scrawl FLQ and ALQ graffiti on walls, and to blow up mailboxes. (The post office made a convenient federal scapegoat then, the way Prime Minister Chrétien does now.)

As far as I was concerned, if increased power for Quebec would transform Canada into Montreal, I was for it.

I had travelled or fled to Quebec for fresh air, to escape the limitations and expectations of my village, unaware that French-Canadians lived in a village too—with its own suffocating embrace of reassurance and necessity. It was fine and dandy for Montreal to provide ethnic relief for repressed Anglos on the run, but that did nothing for the Quebecois from La Tuque.

I was only faintly aware of a cultural revolution not unlike the one I was to experience in 1975 with Theatre Passe Muraille, upon seeing a Canadian story told in a Canadian dialect for the first time in my life. A similar revelation, more profound and on a broader scale, was taking place in 1960s Quebec.

When the "Quiet Revolution" of Lesage (with his Minister of Public Works, René Lévesque) nationalized the electricity industry under the slogan "Maître Chez Nous," it signaled a nationalism well to the left of the traditionalist, Church-dominated variety urged on by the Union Nationale. As well, the plays of Michel Trembley and the songs of Gilles Vigneault and Robert Charlebois treated *joual* no longer as a crude, incorrect dialect of a superior mother tongue, but as oxygen for a distinctive life form.

If you cannot escape your village, one response is to alter the village to suit your needs. By the 1960s, many Quebecers had determined to expel their colonizers in historical order: first to leave would be the divine order of the Catholic Church, followed by the reign of Parisian French, followed by the Dominion of Canada.

Other Quebecers saw things quite differently: If the village was insufficient, what was the point barricading yourself inside, when there was a centre of power you could expand to—called Ottawa? To Pierre Trudeau, Jean Marchand and Gerard Pelletier (called, with typically Canadian irony, "the Three Wise Men"), it was a question of altering *Canada* to suit their needs.

And Prime Minister Pearson wouldn't mind. He wasn't doing anything with it at the time.

Dancing to an Old Tune

But no politician can free the imaginary country from its inherited forms. The feet may move on, but the footprints remain.

We tend to think of political power in terms of the Darwinian fish diagram—in which a small fish is eaten by a bigger fish, which is then eaten by a still bigger fish, and so on up the food chain. But the diagram, implying a progression from small to large, from weak to strong, does not reflect Canada, where the progression goes the other way: The chain is not of one species consuming another, but of one species *imitating* another. In Canada the fish, imitating a larger fish, swallows an apparently smaller fish, which in imitation swallows an apparently still smaller fish, and on down the line until you find the pattern repeated in the executive council of the Moose Jaw Rotary Club.

My village maintained a repressive system of social interaction in which a layer of insulation, masquerading as goodwill, prevented the honest exchange of ideas, while a higher authority—physically absent yet vividly apparent when required—defined our assumptions about the relative importance of things. (My Grandmother, never having heard or read a word of German, burned the Kaiser in effigy in 1914.)

In a colonized culture, the oppressed imitate their oppressors—whomever they may be. Like the chain of family violence, colonial subservience perpetuates itself, as a descending order of majority cultures reflexively act on minorities the way *another* majority culture acted on them. Thus, colonized Anglophones imitate their British masters by patronizing French-Canadians; Quebecers in turn imitate English-Canadians by patronizing the Cree nation; and no doubt the Cree leadership has someone to patronize too.

The situation is complicated by the fact that Canadians have been colonized from more than one direction. English-Canadians historically feel cultural pressure from Britain (this is changing), economic pressure from the United States, and spiritual pressure from the Protestant church. In their own way, French-Canadians too have had patriarchy coming at them from all sides, from an English and American-controlled economy, a culture bowed in the direction of Paris and Hollywood and, far above them all, that immanent engine of authority—the Catholic Church.

Protestantism exerts a nose-to-the-grindstone ethic on the English-Canadian which, together with an aversion to introspection, gives us that lumbering, priggish quality Quebecers love to mock. But there is no political muscle here; the potential demagogue who would harness Protestantism for political gain must borrow his imagery from the American "born again" Baptist movement of Pat Robertson and Jerry Falwell. Try to express the Canadian social gospel in the form of political activity, and you will find yourself stranded on an NDP backbench for life.

Canadian Protestantism exerts little direct political influence because, historically, it represents a flight *from* the brutal effects of British social engineering. No religious leader in the world wields less political power than the Moderator of the United Church of Canada.

The Catholic Church is a different kettle of fish.

The gradual collapse of the Holy Roman Empire in the fourteenth century left only one structural authority to govern the "universal community under God." Only the Church remained to protect what was left of civilization from the rudimentary yet effective social organization of barbarian thugs and robber barons, the Hell's Angels of Lombardy.

Throughout the fifteenth and sixteenth centuries, the Church became the final authority over birth, marriage, death, sex, eating, philosophy and medicine. Not shy about exercising that power, the

Church devised and enforced a system of rules and punishments that went well beyond the expedient running of the village, from the metal contraptions to be screwed onto the thumbs of gossips to the burning of witches and scientists. Daily actions as basic as the cooking of an egg—"During the length of time for saying a *miserere*"—were defined in terms of Church ritual and doctrine. Membership was compulsory. And dissent was dangerous.

This powerful and well-entrenched political instrument did not simply evaporate as European society became more humanist and secular; its paternal structures of imposed conformity remained in the collective memory to be exploited by any political party that seeks to assume a divine mission—such as the Parti Québécois.

It is not difficult to envisage the voluptuary Jacques Parizeau sporting the red vestments of a cardinal; Lucien Bouchard would look impressively severe in the black robes of a Jesuit monk.

The Parti Québécois sings from the Catholic hymnal in several ways. It is patriarchal in structure. It employs a wide variety of tactics in carrying out its holy work. Its message of deliverance (*La Solution*) resonates among the poor and the powerless. It maintains a unified public doctrine, even when specific objectives are unclear and the party swarms internally with intrigue.

Most important, both the Church and the Parti Québécois exert an unspoken moral authority in Quebec, from which dissent is unwise. Even Robert Bourassa, a utilitarian federalist if ever there was one, found it advisable to chant the sovereigntist *miserere* from time to time, during the boiling of an egg.

Nor is the Parti Québécois without its own pageant of martyrs, patron saints, Judases and demons.

Angels of Deliverance

Born in Cambellton, New Brunswick and trained as a war correspondent for the American armed forces, René Lévesque fits the profile of both a Catholic saint and the hero of an American Western: the charismatic peasant who rallies the citizens, overthrows the forces of evil, frees the village, then rides off into the sunset, leaving the villagers to live in peace, happily ever after.

Like the saint and the sheriff, Lévesque faced stiff competition—from Pierre Trudeau, who fit quite a different mythic profile.

Trudeau's role was that of the charismatic aristocrat who uses inherited privilege as an instrument of liberation, empowering the villagers by taking over the empire on their behalf: a heroic model he shared with Zorro, Constantine the Great and, turning to his mother's side of the family, Robert the Bruce.

In 1968, Pierre Trudeau became Prime Minister of Canada, and René Lévesque formed the Parti Québécois. Trudeau became Pope, and René Lévesque became St. Stephen—his body pierced by a hundred hyphens.

But in the village, surprisingly, not much changed.

Martyred by the Hyphen

A TV personality, hence a believer in popular slogans and images, Lévesque coined the term *sovereignty-association* early, as a rhetorical balm for Quebecers' practical fears; despite a thriving imaginary country, the prospect of a tiny French-speaking nation-state in North America flourishing amid the hurly-burly of global politics and trade wars seemed chancy at best.

Nobody knew what "sovereignty-association" meant. The term was an empty container for the contradictory emotions of sovereign pride and secure dependence, designed to become an attractive brand name for the PQ product; a piece of all-purpose, feel-good rhetoric along the lines of "The Lord is my shepherd" and "We do it all for you."

The trouble was, although it accurately expressed the dual aspirations of Quebecers, sovereignty-association seemed like a weasel word when compared to the simple and direct term *independence*—a slogan previously marketed by the *Rassemblement pour l'independence national.* Trained in Jesuit schools and not fussy about his debating tactics, Trudeau exploited the contradictory sentiments expressed by sovereignty-association to full advantage, tearing the hyphen out and releasing the fear that had brought it about.

Lévesque had no effective reply other than some theme songs by Gilles Vigneault—and even the lyrics to the classic imaginary anthem "Mon Pays" were not as vague in the real world as sovereignty-association.

Following the referendum defeat in 1980, Lévesque the media

icon changed his style, abandoning the pugnacious stance of the bantamweight fighter for the resigned shrug of the martyr, together with a forgiving tilt of the head and a gentle shuffle from left to right. Even his smoking became more reflective—the puffing of a man who has been warned about cancer but knows it's too late to stop now.

It seemed as though Trudeau, the non-smoker, would live forever. His shrug was nothing like Lévesque's shrug. Trudeau shrugged because he could not be bothered to talk to you. It was his way of telling people who disagreed with him that they were irrelevant; they simply did not matter.

Ironically, Trudeau went on to market a set of even more bewildering, contradictory, hyphenated policies—known as bilingualism, biculturalism, and the notwithstanding clause. While sovereignty-association seemed an ungainly bird, Trudeau's binary experiments were not going to fly at all.

What Trudeau failed to see or acknowledge, linear thinker that he was, was that sovereignty-association can be read in two directions: The sovereigntist reads it from left to right, while the federalist reads it from right to left. The two sides are not at war. The difference between federalist and separatist in Quebec is a matter of nuance.

Moreover, the empire Trudeau took over when he became Prime Minister was not an empire at all, but another series of villages, with the same needs and fears—the need for self-definition, the fear of disappearance—as the French felt. If there are "two nations" in Canada, they are not French and English; if applicable at all, the term describes the gap between how Canadians see themselves and how they are reflected by their government.

This meant that, once in Ottawa, there was nobody for Zorro to rescue, and nobody to rescue them from.

Star Gazing

If Quebecers saw Trudeau as a Constantine or a Judas—depending on their affiliation—in English Canada he was the object of *Trudeaumania*.

Although derived from the term *Beatlemania* (like the many derivatives of *Watergate*), Trudeau's appeal to Canadians was closer to that of the androgynous Mick Jagger, throwing kisses and flowers while singing "Let's Spend the Night Together." An instinctive media manipulator, his political genius was to invent a language to describe Quebec's cultural and political emancipation that perfectly matched the Aquarian language of generational emancipation—a message made popular by The Doors and the Jefferson Airplane. Every word Trudeau uttered had two meanings: one for the English, and one for the French.

The 1968 Liberal slogan—"The Just Society"—typified his genius for double-talk.

For one summer I worked as an incompetent labourer for the Cook & Leach Construction Company, renovating the Bell Telephone building on de la Gauchetière Street. Even I could not help but notice that unskilled and semi-skilled labourers—welders, carpenters, pipefitters and drywallers—spoke French while, at the level of foreman and above, English was the language of choice. Imagine what The Just Society must have implied to Francophones who worked for Cook & Leach.

To English Canada on the other hand, The Just Society was pure Bob Dylan. Power to the People. Give Peace a Chance. We Shall Overcome. Such expressions may have had meaning when applied to the Vietnam War and the civil rights movement, but by the time they crossed the 49th Parallel they had become political fashion accessories, advertising text to accompany the rose in the lapel and kisses all around.

Derivative maybe, but for the first time in our history Canadians boasted a Prime Minister who was young and interesting and "continental," who mocked British conventions and attracted American celebrities. To English Canada, Pierre Trudeau made a dazzling hood ornament, proclaiming to the world that we were not as dull as our reputation, that we drove a vintage Mercedes and not a Ford.

The fact that both French and English voted for the same man lent an appearance of unanimity to the 1968 Liberal sweep, when in truth it represented two entirely different responses to the same symbolic language. Canada had become bilingual, in more ways than one.

If only we had not all fallen for him as hard as we did. If only Trudeau had remained a cerebral pundit and had not transformed himself overnight into Mick Jagger.

If only the West had voted characteristically for Bob Stanfield, maintaining the delicate equilibrium of contradiction and ambivalence that characterizes Canadian politics at its best. Stanfield epitomized Anglo *niceness*—modest, musty and wise, like *The Globe and Mail* before it discovered monetarist economic theology.

But the media, wearing bell-bottoms and beads that year, were with Trudeau all the way. A newspaper photograph depicting Stanfield fumbling a football, eyeglasses askew on his long nose, lips pursed in a hoser grimace, seemed to epitomize everything English-Canadians hated about themselves and wanted to escape, everything they lacked that Trudeau seemed to possess. Stanfield, and in a way the constituency he represented, became a national joke. (Stanfield caught several footballs that day with perfect grace. He only missed one.)

Once in power, Trudeau's bicameral presence held even through the October Crisis of 1970, when a kidnapping and murder provided the rationale for the jailing of Quebec nationalists and union leaders willy-nilly, without warrants or evidence. Like a Third World capital during a coup attempt, troop carriers and tanks rumbled down the streets of Montreal, and Zorro removed his mask to reveal the sneer of an emperor.

But as long as the troops were on television and not the streets of Toronto, Trudeau could still keep the Anglos guessing. When he announced the suspension of constitutional rights on national TV, his thinning hair fell well below his shoulders—he looked like a member of The Grateful Dead in a suit. The message may have been that of a South American dictator, but the medium was pure flower power.

For a man whose whole life was a planned scenario of Greek perfection out of a boy's book (intellect, athletics, wild oats and power), it could hardly have been an accident that he chose "Pierre Elliott" over five given names: thus, to Quebecers he was "Pierre," while Ontarians could find comfort in the ever-so-Anglo "Elliott." And whatever his motives at the time, it was of no small tactical advantage in English Canada to have married Margaret Sinclair of West Vancouver, augmenting the youthful image of a man well into middle age, and silencing persistent rumours about his sexual preferences.

Politically, Trudeau promised to create a country in which English and French counterbalanced each other, in which each culture provided a Montreal for the other. To French-Canadians he promised an escape beyond the borders of Quebec, while to English-Canadians he said: "The state has no place in the bedrooms of the nation." It was the first time Anglos had heard *that* one.

In the end, of course, he could deliver none of these things— because nobody wanted them. For villagers in Quebec, the nation-state Canada provided an area of certain agreement. Opposition to the Anglos, like the weather, was a safe topic that enabled Quebecers to avoid the risks involved in confronting their differences.

Canada is the device that enables French-Canadians, like their Anglo counterparts, to see and not to see at the same time. Thanks to English Canada, St. René Lévesque could kill a man with his car on Côte de Neige after a festive evening, and escape dire political consequences.

Trudeau may have repatriated the Constitution, but he was not going to be able to persuade Quebecers to give up the hyphen, and the mobility it provides.

In the same way, he could never secure a Charter of Rights and Freedoms that guaranteed "inalienable" individual rights, the way the American Constitution does. That is simply not the Canadian way—French or English. The Canadian way is to qualify those rights at every turn with hyphenated "notwithstanding clauses"—just in case those rights should one day prove inconvenient, or entail social responsibilities we do not wish to shoulder.

Similarly, Brian Mulroney, another Quebecer, seeking "reconciliation" through the Meech Lake Accord, found himself confounded by hyphens at every turn; in negotiating the Free Trade Agreement with the United States, even Canada's cultural sovereignty had to be qualified by "notwithstanding clauses"—just in case the right to self-definition should carry too high a price tag.

In this area Canadians are exactly alike, French and English, from sea to sea. We are determined to maintain two minds at all times. We will not be pinned down to a course of action that does not provide for an escape route. We will never be manoeuvred into opting for one side of the hyphen and rejecting the other.

This stance is nowhere more evident than in that marvellous Québécois expression, *we will wear our suspenders **and** our belt.*

Disastrous Majorities

My Grandfather used to warn against majority governments carried to victory by contradictory expectations. Desperate to give everyone what they want, they give Canada something nobody wants.

He was referring to the John Diefenbaker sweep, but it could well have been those Trudeau majorities that treated us to bilingualism, the War Measures Act, our repatriated Constitution and the Charter of Rights and Freedoms—even though Canadians, French and English, had never expressed a desire for any of those things.

Or he could just as easily have been referring to the Progressive Conservative majorities under Brian Mulroney. Here was another Quebecer whose back-to-back majorities treated us to such popular measures as a trade deal with the USA, a failed constitutional accord, and a general tax on goods and services that turned every self-employed Canadian into a tax collector.

As did Trudeau, Brian Mulroney sported two public masks to accommodate the national schizophrenia: to the English he presented a Reaganite vision of corporate North America, while to the French he was the boy from the shop floor who made it to Management.

As they did with Trudeau, both English and French Canada voted for Mulroney—for entirely different reasons. The West and Southern Ontario voted for the party that promised an end to Trudeau's economic policies, while Quebecers, seething over Trudeau's constitutional repatriation—another Judas-like betrayal of St. René Lévesque—voted Tory after Mulroney co-opted the independentiste movement, attracting Marcel Masse and other Union Nationale types into the federal party, often by turning a blind eye to legal blots on the resumé.

Mimicking Trudeau's duplicity if not his subtlety, Mulroney spoke one language to English Canada (the language of negotiation and of neoconservative economics), and another to Quebec (the language of political and economic independence). To Quebecers, Mulroney handled *joual* like René Lévesque's smooth cousin from the States; to English Canada, he spoke with the soothing reassurance of a late-night FM host on an easy listening station. If Trudeau was Mick Jagger, Mulroney was Frank Sinatra.

The genius of the bilateral trade deal with the United States was that, as an issue, it fed Western alienation, Eastern malaise and Sovereigntist ambition all at once, giving each of those populist sentiments a continental, neoconservative spin.

The dropping of tariffs would provide Quebec with a mammoth North-South trading partner to release the economy from dependence on English Canada. Instead of left-leaning René Lévesque, the peasant hero, the sword of independence was to be taken up by the Bombardier Péquistes, ready to take lunch with the world.

To the West, the trade deal promised to loosen the western provinces' economic subservience to Quebec and Ontario; meanwhile in Ontario, although resistance to the deal was strongest there, "Free Trade" became a Bay Street Charles Atlas fantasy in which a weakling hero, tired of having sand kicked in his face, becomes lean and muscular thanks to the dynamic tension of laissez-faire competition, ready to compete on a "level playing field" with the Americans.

Whether it was a vote for Western enfranchisement, pinstripe machismo or *independence*, all of Canada voted for Brian Mulroney, and the Progressive Conservative party swept to power with a self-contradictory mandate that could never be fulfilled.

Meanwhile, with federal encouragement, Quebec laid the groundwork for a new brand of sovereignty with a redesigned, multinational label. Led by Jacques Parizeau, an economist trained at the London School of Economics who is fond of the expression "by Jove!" (Bourassa was a Harvard man), the new Parti Québécois is far more comfortable with the traditional levers of Roman Catholic conservatism than René Lévesque ever was. Highly paternalistic, more than willing to step on heretics, and with limited patience for the principle of one-person one-vote democracy, the mission of the Parti Québécois is to forge a contained social hierarchy in which a unilingual labour force (with limited negotiating strength) is led by a bilingual, globally-competitive managerial class who live in Westmount, whose children attend English private schools and American universities to prepare them for inherited privilege and power.

Sounds rather like the Cook & Leach Construction Company to me.

The Bloc Québécois has a good deal in common with the Reform Party, in that it seeks to return to an edited vision of the past that is more to its liking. If Parizeau and Bouchard have their way, Quebecers will return to the village and lock the gates; if Reformers have their way, so will we. Neither will have a Montreal to escape to; communication between villages will be filtered through the ideological strainer of a captive village media. English-Canadian television will feature hairy students, burning the Prime Minister in effigy; Quebecers will be treated to more footage of Polyester-clad Anglos stomping on the Quebec flag.

But it would be extremely uncharacteristic for Canadians, French or English, to be persuaded by politicians to remove traditional items of haberdashery and to risk being caught with their pants down. Already the Bombardier Péquistes scramble for qualifiers and notwithstanding clauses—such as the retention of Canadian currency and even Canadian citizenship in an "independent" Quebec—while Bombardier's chairman has rediscovered a passion for Canadian unity on the Montreal luncheon circuit.

For any political party, the business community is a flighty mistress at the best of times. The Parti Québécois should have stuck with the poets.

However, although Canada will probably survive the current "crisis"—if indeed any nation-state survives current global trends—we are in for a testy time. We will be clenching our teeth a bit tighter than usual for the next little while.

Even in an atmosphere of goodwill, negotiating with Quebec tends to elicit paranoia in English Canada. Their tactical voting patterns lead Anglos to suspect we are dealing with an opposing team equipped with ESP. Quebecers, when buttonholed at random for a clip on the evening news, seem instinctively to know exactly what to say that will alarm the Anglos. It is as though Quebecers secretly consult specialists who tell them what to say on TV to strengthen their hand at the bargaining table.

Paranoia is further enhanced by the fact that English-Canadians are only too aware of Quebecers' savvy and style. They see Quebec movies; they watch their own television shows; they listen to their own records. Gilles Vigneault can sell out the Théâtre de Maisonneuve for *a year.*

Taken altogether, it all leads English-Canadians to habitually suspect them of putting one over on us, with the reverse snobbery country bumpkins feel for city slickers—the same sentiment that leads traditional NDP supporters to vote Reform out of sheer bile.

But in the end, one way or another, we are not going to agree either to unite or to separate. Negotiations between English and French Canada will continue before and after the next Quebec referendum, whenever it occurs, whatever the result, on and on until kingdom come.

Up for Air (Reprise)

During the 1980s, a musical I wrote, called *Rock and Roll*, was translated into *joual* and produced by a small theatre company in Quebec City. The musical is about a band in a small Canadian town, how its members deal with the limitations of that culture. The production was skillful, and its Quebec setting seemed relatively effortless. Even the music sounded indigenous, as the players pushed the beat in the style of Les Classels and Les Eccentriques.

I spent a week with the theatre company and was treated like a visiting dignitary, although there was some muttering as to whether the show was *misogynistique*. After a few days my hosts grew comfortable, or possibly bored, with my presence, and ceased to speak English for my benefit.

As I nursed my beer and listened with my rudimentary French, their conversations sounded achingly familiar: Who said what to whom, about whom? Whose efforts to conceal their age or inexperience or sexuality had made them a laughing-stock? Who had been caught in a compromising situation? Whose ambitions marked them for disaster? Who did somebody or other think they were?

Ten years later, on a visit to Alberta, I ran into the former director of that Quebec theatre company. He had recently moved to Edmonton, lured by the dynamic of its international fringe festival, which had become the largest event of its type in the world.

He looked and talked like a man who had come up for air.

THE EXTRA GANG:
THE NATIONAL DREAM, REMEMBERED

You Are What You Recall

Memories are treacherous. They contain truth and lies. They provide meaning and they take it away. They bring Quebecers together ("Je me souviens"), and tear Yugoslavians apart.

Most of us live according to a model of ourselves in which we are the way we are because of the way "the world" treated us yesterday. Hindsight makes sense of everything by placing the world "out there," as an implied Other, thinking and acting upon an imagined Self.

Responding to the world in its costume as hero, victim or villain, this imagined, romanticized inner Self inspires feelings of pride, resentment and guilt, but really it is all happening to somebody else. The part of us watching—whoever that is, peering out from underneath the eyelids—remains unexamined and safe.

Only we are not safe.

Just as a novelist revises a character's biography according to the inner demands of plot and structure, we revise our past lives according to how we need to view ourselves now—to "make sense" of the way things turned out. But as time goes by and inexplicable events grow in number, it becomes an increasing strain to "make sense" of things, and our ongoing inner narrative from birth to the present reveals itself, increasingly, as a work of fiction.

As we get older, memories, like friends, become more numerous but less reliable; more apt to tell us what we want to hear than what we need to know.

The most valuable memories are those in which we remember ourselves, not as heroes opposed to the world, but as part of a world, a collective event in which we existed as supporting players. With a smaller stake in the plot, we need not alter the script to fit our personal melodrama. We can let the inexplicable remain so. The urge to distort is less imperative, and the memory is more apt to be reliable and true.

The two Canadian generations before me are still haunted by their collective war experience, humming within. They do not know what to make of that memory and, as NFB and CBC producers periodically discover, they do not want to be told what to make of it. What they do know is that the war was real and that they want their memory of it to remain real. That is what Remembrance Day is for—keeping the memory real. The minute of silence is not only for the dead, it is a symbolic moment in which present conflict is silenced, in memory of a time when Canadians did not feel separate, but united in something worth living and dying for.

My generation has not done such a good job remembering. The late 1960s was a time when, with the naïveté of teenagers, we thought we were about to vault onto a new platform of human evolution. It was beyond our imagining that, years later, we would be wearing ties and high-heeled shoes just like our parents, competing for that extra piece of pie.

Today, if we try, we can summon up images of Mountain Street and Yorkville and 4th Avenue, of Rochdale Free University, the Company of Young Canadians, Opportunities For Youth and the Committee for an Independent Canada. But these images easily become confused with better-televised American ones—Vietnam and Civil Rights and Haight-Ashbury—so that none of it seems real anymore.

Perhaps we need a Remembrance Day too.

Still, everyone has personal memories that retain their power despite their misuse as propaganda, despite bad movies about Dieppe and bad songs about Woodstock—memories of times in which we temporarily lost ourselves in something more significant, felt joined with people we would normally avoid; in which we felt part of something real, even if we did not know quite what it was.

Lacking a film industry, with a television industry overly drawn to ratings and a publishing industry overly drawn to "art," Canadians traditionally maintain their collective memories through storytelling over kitchen tables and in Legion bars. Every village has its storytellers who can gather a crowd, who evoke events and people and make them real. Not only do individual memories stay alive this way, but the memories of others reinforce them. Related memories form a collage that sustains the imaginary country in the minds of its citizens—even when its political existence is in flux. Like the Jews during the diaspora, we create a mental panorama for ourselves that cannot be destroyed because it all comes from the same mysterious collective source.

That is why a national culture is so powerful and so difficult to erase, why the imaginary Canadian will haunt the continent long after the customs depots have shut down.

As we undergo the process of "globalization," vivid, inexplicable memories will persist in the minds of our grandchildren to ensure that Canada will outlive us all, that Canada will outlive Canada.

If we do not take these memories into account, they are going to cause a lot of grief.

Let me tell you about my summer of 1965, spent working on a CNR extra gang near Esterhazy, Saskatchewan, when I first experienced the national dream.

The New World

The train glided over the distant horizon, leaving me standing on the wooden platform in the buzzing heat of a Saskatchewan summer, exposed as a lightening rod under that enormous globe of a sky. I had never before seen so much sky while on land.

"Cutarm," said the letter in my suitcase. I had never heard of Cutarm. Not far from Esterhazy, the conductor had explained—but I had no idea where Esterhazy was, either. Esterhazy was near the Qu'Appelle River—never heard of the Qu'Appelle River. Orientation was impossible, place names were markers of smoke, yet here I was.

How typical of train travel—the experience of geography as an immediate sensual presence, disorienting yet vivid, with no imaginable overview. On a plane you become blind and deaf, hurtling through space with plugs in your ears, glancing down occasionally at the quilt beneath the clouds, aloof and superior to the earth, seeing nothing.

How many days had I spent on that train? Long enough for that unmistakable train smell to permeate my clothes, for the platform to feel strangely still under my feet. Long enough to feel part of the train subculture, of life in that moving village, with its own government, bylaws and police force, and its ever shifting population.

I picked up my suitcase, noting the unaccustomed ease of movement, a cooperative stillness to everything with no need for hand grips to keep my balance. Two monumental red grain elevators towered above me. They shimmered in the sun, yet remained in one place—they did not whiz by in a momentary blur. I had arrived in Gerald, the closest town to the old Cutarm railway siding. I trudged up the deserted, unpaved road to the Gerald Hotel. Animals lurked in the shade, out of the midday heat—dogs, cats, and a domestic cow.

The Gerald Hotel was a shabby expedient, a means to a provincial liquor licence, not a business in itself. Inside the beer parlour, shrouded in tobacco haze, damp men crouched over small, round, pastel terry cloth-covered tables, nursing a strange, salmon-coloured beverage that turned out to be beer and tomato juice—a drink sometimes known as a "redeye." Their faces were all but invisible, obscured by peaked caps with tractor advertisements on the forehead. One man removed his cap to scratch: It was as though he had been dipped in whitewash, head first, creating a precise line above the eyebrow.

Most of these men appeared meaty and prone to high blood pressure—bloated bellies extended in front as a convenient shelf for crossed forearms like fallen logs; a few were brown and skinny, neck cords standing out like wire, with the spiny anatomical efficiency we now associate with longevity.

They watched me as I sat down, rolling Sportsman tobacco into Vogue papers and murmuring warily in Slavic and Ukrainian. I waited, thinking that, if I had travelled this far *east* from Nova Scotia, and not west, I would now be in the Soviet Union, not Canada.

Could Russia seem more alien than the Gerald Hotel?

Frontier College

The assistant foreman from the extra gang stared down at me from under a striped cloth railway cap, its peak at an angle exactly parallel to his long, peeling aquiline nose. He looked like a brown crow. In the glare of his suspicion, I felt unspecifically guilty.

"Frontier College?" His lips never budged; a moist cigarette waggled up and down slightly.

"No," I replied. "Actually, I have a friend from Frontier College. He told me about the extra gang. I'm just here to work."

The mouth tightened, the cigarette curled slightly. I should not have complicated the issue; should not have used the word "actually."

Back home in Nova Scotia, where everyone remembers your uncle, I was a middle-class youngster, a safe, known quantity. I was not used to seeing suspicion glaring back at me. Other people were the strangers, not me.

As we drove to camp in an orange CNR pickup truck, I explained that I had applied to Frontier College (a program for university students to teach literacy in the wilderness), but was rejected as too stupid, immature, and feckless; not Frontier College material.

However, there was nothing to stop my becoming an itinerant labourer myself. A university acquaintance (Rick was Frontier College material, the pick of the litter he was) wrote that the CNR was taking men on for the extra gang—a work unit of unskilled labourers with no seniority and no future with the firm.

With my savings I bought a coach-class ticket to Winnipeg, then another up the CNR line to Cutarm, where the extra gang was assembling to lay track at the world's largest potash mine in Esterhazy. Eighty dollars a week, plus a bed and all you could eat. There I joined a loose collection of men who did not know one another and did not want to know me. Mobile labour means distrust and suspicion which, in the extra gang, hardened into a culture of solitude.

I had entered a Frontier College of my own, a school of entry-level Canadiana, and I had plenty to learn: Do not touch another man's bunk or possessions; do not ask his last name or his home address; do not make unnecessary eye contact; do not try to borrow anything, not even a smoke. These rules were never stated; there was never any need. We all knew what they were.

The Servants' Entrance

Most of my colleagues were "new Canadians," family men gaining admittance to the national dream the hard, yet honourable way—not through the main foyer, reserved for high rolling entrepreneurs and degreed professionals, nor by the back door, which was occasionally opened a crack to admit refugees and charity cases, then quickly slammed shut again. No, these men were entering Canada through the servants' entrance, through hard work and painful savings. That entrance is still open today for queues of Filipino nannies, Korean cashiers at the 7-11, and Sikh parking lot attendants with degrees in chemical engineering.

With the accumulated earnings of a couple of summers on the extra gang, a man could amass a sufficient stake to open a corner grocery store, the favoured entry-level enterprise leading to better things. Then would come a bigger grocery store, a small apartment building, even a restaurant. The sky was the limit in a country like Canada.

Others, like Duda, the white-haired Frenchman—compact and handsome, with serene, aquamarine eyes—were content to leave the upward mobility to the next generation. Duda cleaned offices and worked at construction jobs all winter to scrape together and maintain a middle-class standard of living in suburban Winnipeg. His daughter attended nursing school: Did she know that Duda paid for her education by spending his summers laying railway ties, miles from home?

Then there were the "new Canadians" who had arrived years before and never made it out of the cloakroom. Unmarried or formerly-married, spirits broken beyond repair, they had given up on the national dream. Instead they had reduced life to the basics, then tightened the wrench some more.

Washed out like long-term convicts, these stoic shadows seldom spoke, never read, and never drank unless it was to disappear furtively for a desperate, week-long binge. Before and after the day's work they remained in camp, eating, smoking, sleeping; and shaving—a pensive, languid affair with a straight razor that could take a half-hour. They sat on railway ties and rolled cigarettes one after the other, their elbows resting on their knees. When they ran short of makings, they sent Harold the timekeeper into town—out of fear not laziness, for they toiled with dogged diligence. Terrified of unfamiliar places and spaces, when the summer ended they would rent rooms in Winnipeg boarding houses to spend the winter in suspension, hibernating and rolling cigarettes until the timekeeper knocked on their door the following spring.

In my sophomoric mind I referred to these men as the hungry ghosts.

John Adam

One of the ghosts did not fit the pattern: Adam the water boy, an ironic designation, for Adam looked at least seventy, tall and gaunt, wearing what remained of a dark blue 1940s suit, a straw hat and Tommy Douglas rimless spectacles. Nobody knew his surname, which was typical, except that Adam didn't know it himself. The timekeeper had listed him as "John Adam," only to fill a blank on the employment form.

The word around the camp was that Adam had stowed away on a ship from Russia around the turn of the century, and had worked on the railway gangs ever since until, long before anyone could remember and out of deference to his steady service, he became a kind of company mascot with the position of water boy.

The years had taken their toll on his mind more than his body. Adam's Russian had faded away from disuse, while his English, never fluent, had contracted to the one broken phrase he still required in his line of work.

"Dhlink! Ice code dhlink!" he would proclaim as he made his rounds under the merciless sun, a full pail of water in each glove, consonants sputtering over a perfect set of his own teeth. He was an old man but also a child, radiant with health, innocent and easy to delight. Curiously, Adam did not roll cigarettes. Perhaps he had forgotten how.

Among the extra gang he was held aside and regarded tolerantly as an amiable simpleton and the subject of one more unwritten rule: You did not tease him, no matter how drunk or bored you became, and he who mistreated Adam cashed out the next day.

For three months I lived with Adam and six other men in one of several boxcars equipped for the purpose with barracks-style double bunks, a washstand and a window. Bram, the embittered

Polish herbalist, was in an upper corner: The roof beams provided shelf space for his sealer jars of yellow glop, which proved to be a surprisingly powerful healing agent when I drove a picaroon into my left instep. Below Bram was a future Portuguese grocer, and another one across from him—so that the two could play cards seated on the edge of their bunks. The top bunk opposite Bram contained an apple-cheeked ghost with waxen hair and crystal eyes, the ideal rural grandfather for a life insurance advertisement, were it not for the eerie silence that surrounded him like smoke. Two more ghosts with frightened, rodent faces occupied the centre bunk. I slept in the lower bunk beneath Adam, who vaulted above me each night like a teenager, and was serenely snoring in a matter of seconds.

The regimen never varied. Six days a week we awoke at six, ate breakfast in the dining car, then boarded the flatbed truck to the work site, where we picked things up and put things down all morning. The flatbed took us back to camp for lunch, then back into the sweltering heat for the afternoon. Then home again, where we shaved at the washstand by our car entrance, ate dinner in the dining car, and lay exhausted in our bunks. Enormous meals were prepared by a Mrs. O'Brien: about sixty, she was implausibly rumoured to be having an affair with Foster, the crow I had encountered in the beer parlour on my first day.

The shared routine inspired no *esprit de corps*. The Portuguese preferred to chat to one another in their own language. Bram's professional certificate as a Polish herbalist had been disallowed in Canada years earlier, and he complained about it with wearying predictability. The ghosts preferred to speak to no one at all. And Adam didn't know how to say anything except: "Dhlink! Ice code dhlink!"

Ant Work

The work itself was the sort of thing ants do—ants with creosote-encrusted gloves, picking up heavy objects and carrying them about. When laying the wooden railway ties, we picked them up two men to a tie and placed them in a row on the roadbed, up and down, over and over again, soaked with sweat and dust and creosote.

Laying down the steel rails was far worse: about twenty men would line up two by two in a chain gang-like procession, each holding one handle of a large, specially-made pair of tongs. At a signal from the foreman, everyone lifted—not too lightly, because they could tell if you failed to pull your weight, nor too heavily, unless you wanted a back injury or a hernia. A rail is sufficiently heavy that its movement cannot be influenced by any one man, creating a fine line between enthusiasm and rupture. On the extra gang you could sustain one of two ruptures—either you "busted a gut" or you "broke your bag." With either of these self-explanatory diagnoses, your railway career was at an end.

We worked in swarms in the boiling sun, the grinding tedium punctuated by that welcome refrain—"Dhlink! Ice code dhlink!"

At first I thought Adam had been created water boy as a sop to old age—until I was told to carry a couple of those pails for a half-hour and found I could no longer lift my arms. The Esterhazy work site covered a good many acres; no wonder he ate six eggs for breakfast.

A Canadian Miracle

For conversation after work hours I turned to Harold the melancholy timekeeper. High school-educated and unlucky in love, a series of women had thrown Harold out on his ear—usually a couple of days after he had paid off the fridge and stove. A lonely, tentative, ungainly man, Harold collected pulp periodicals on occult phenomena, rolled cigarettes, kept the work records, performed minor first aid, and maintained a fiduciary regard for the men he had shaken from their Winnipeg boarding houses the previous spring.

One night I drank too much beer and tomato juice, and tumbled noisily out the door of our boxcar while taking a piss in the dead of night, to a chorus of "Go to bed!" in several European dialects. When I bragged to Harold about the incident (you brag about such things as a youth), he frowned: "The boys need their sleep. If one of them complains, I'll have you fired."

Through Harold I heard the news about Adam the water boy. Apparently the CNR had been trying to take a reading on Adam's precise age for several years, since he had no memory of the statistic himself. Although letters to the Soviet embassy in Ottawa had produced nothing, this exercise in international diplomacy had become a minor bureaucratic thrill at the local office of the CNR. Every six months or so, some bored clerk would fire off an inquiry about a Mr. John Adam, language Russian, who had stowed away on a prerevolutionary navy ship around 1900.

That summer a miracle occurred in the form of a curt reply from the Soviets, confirming a dog-eared report on a stowaway with the pseudonym Adam, a young peasant expelled from a Russian merchant ship in Montreal. The birth date contained in the letter made Adam a youthful eighty-two.

The salient thing about that fact, according to Harold, was that the CNR and the Canadian Government both owed Adam seventeen years in back pension money—sixty-five being the compulsory retirement age. Plus interest. Compounded. CNR management promptly sent a letter acknowledging the debt: A cheque would be forwarded in the mail.

Then a series of dogged, very Canadian miracles began to unfold around John Adam. The institutions and governments of some lesser country might have evaded their obligation, shrouding his case in bureaucratic obfuscation until Adam's death made payments unnecessary. But this was the CNR, and this was Canada, whose institutions rested on a foundation of inflexible, methodical, Celtic honesty. The water boy was a comparatively wealthy man.

Then the bank letters started coming in.

Did we have a John Adam in our work unit? Because a John Adam had deposited $2000 in a savings account in the Yorkton Bank in 1921, with such abiding faith in the Canadian banking system that the investment had slipped his mind entirely. And—yet another miracle—the Canadian banking system had not let him down. Adam's money had rested comfortably in their vaults year after year, accumulating interest at the going rate, compounded.

More letters came from banks—from Saskatoon, Prince Albert, from as far away as Calgary. When Harold factored in his pension, savings and compounded interest, John Adam possessed slightly over a quarter of a million 1965 dollars.

But he was no longer the water boy. With his company cheque came his retirement notice, together with expressions of thanks and congratulations on a job well done.

Harold asked Bram, the Polish herbalist who had some Russian, to explain the situation to Adam and to ask him what he planned to do with his money. Adam's reply was remarkably succinct and well thought-out: He wanted to buy a TV. He wanted to go for walks during the day. He wanted to drink beer in the evening. He never wanted to work again.

Around noon one day, Adam climbed into the box of the same orange CNR pickup truck I had arrived in months before, wearing his suit, straw hat, spectacles and a clean shirt. The foreman and Harold the timekeeper shook his hand in turn, otherwise nothing was made of the fact that he would never be seen again. In a transitional fraternity like the extra gang where men disappeared forever on a weekly basis, this was standard practice.

Not a word was uttered by the ghosts. They climbed onto the back of the flatbed truck for the afternoon shift and stood waiting in silence, rolling cigarettes, all eyes staring at this singular embodiment of the national dream come true: health, serenity and a nice big pension. A dream that had failed to materialize for them.

From the back of the orange pickup Adam looked at me, standing in the boxcar doorway, about to climb down from the home we had shared. He waved, smiling like a child with his perfect teeth. I waved back with a manufactured grin. The engine revved and the pickup lurched up the hill toward Gerald. Adam held on the side of the truck for balance and called out once again: "Ice code dhlink!" to no one in particular, waving to all of us one last time with his free hand. Then he disappeared over the horizon, into that enormous Saskatchewan sky.

That was when I noticed Adam's ancient, creosote-encrusted work gloves, sitting on the washstand by the sink—deliberately, precisely, side by side.

Adam knew the culture of the extra gang as well as anyone. I believe he had left his gloves there on purpose, fully aware that, such was the ethic of solitude, no man would touch them for the rest of the season.

And nobody did. Adam's gloves lay there on the washstand by the sink like a pair of ancient, disembodied hands, as immovable as though they had been cast in concrete. No man could wash, shave or—significantly—get a drink of water, without taking a good look at Adam's gloves.

Even now, over a quarter of a century later, in my house in Vancouver, with two children asleep upstairs and two cars in the garage, the memory remains clear.

GETTING VAGUE FOR
THE TWENTY-FIRST CENTURY:
A VIEW OF THE CULTURAL LANDSCAPE

A Figment of the Imagination

You may or may not be aware that I am a "West Coast Writer," although I am occasionally identified as a "Maritimer"—even if I have scarcely written a thing in Nova Scotia and have not lived there in over twenty-five years.

For a heady, urban period in the 1970s, I became the "Maritime-born Toronto Writer," a label that still applies from time to time. If I ever land an artist-in-residence sinecure at the University of Saskatoon, I have an outside chance of becoming a "Prairie Writer" as well. I am not ready to be a "Canadian Writer," though—you have to leave the country for that.

What information do these signifiers impart? Does a regional label bring about an understanding that the word "Canadian" fails to provide? Do people exclaim, "I see! He went to school in the Maritimes!" Or, "Now I understand! He occupies a Vancouver bungalow! He gardens! He rides a bicycle!"

No, I suspect that these regional identifications are part of an old mental habit, an inbred disposition to diminish the collective imagination—our ongoing inner sense of ourselves as comprising "a people"—and to confine it to isolated hunks of geography.

Regional labels provide an avoidance mechanism for people who do not want to face the fact that we also occupy an imaginary space called Canada: that collection of memories and shared observations about life that have accrued on the northern half of the North American continent over the past century and a half.

The imaginary Canada is not a piece of real estate, nor a collection of "resources," any more than it is the CBC or the RCMP. Nor does this continuous, evolving inner nation depend upon the governing party of the day, nor even upon the existence of the 49th Parallel.

But if there is a meaner confinement than identification by region, it is to be identified as a *North American*. Regionalism may be unhealthy to the imaginary Canada, but continentalism can be downright toxic.

Everywhere you look these days, in print and on screen, you encounter "North America," as in "The North American marketplace," "The North American Free Trade Agreement" and, more recently and ominously, "North American culture": Yet another label to keep our imaginary country under wraps, out of sight and mind. The imaginary country unnerves the business community and the government equally; unlike tracts of real estate, it cannot be bought or sold or negotiated.

The fashionable assumption at work seems to be that the collective psyche of a group of people (whether a nation, a province or a village) follows the choices of its business and political elites; that "free trade," the "communication revolution" and the "free market" under US leadership will cause the nation-state to become less of a factor in our lives, and its citizens will become more "free"—a triumphant extension of the 1776 American Revolution in which white males (those who owned property and slaves at least) declared themselves similarly "free."

Sounds like religion to me.

According to this scenario, Canadians can look forward to shiny new afterlives as general North Americans, dancing with our former Mexican counterparts around the US maypole, having shed our outdated, subsidized national skins like garter snakes in spring, ready to greet the world in a bright new coat:

"Hi! I'm North American!"

Good God.

Where Is Here and Where Is There

In joining the perpetual debate over the present and future of Canada, the immediate temptation is to assume the role of an amateur television commentator—a savvy Machiavellian chess player looking down at the country and musing about where "it" is going. For some reason we seem to feel that a red blotch on a map (perhaps the big school map with the Rowntree's Chocolate ad in the corner) embodies something solid and observable.

We forget that God did not call this land Canada: Jacques Cartier did, and he had scarcely ventured ten miles from the St. Lawrence at the time. Canada was in Cartier's head, and Canada now is in ours—an internally-generated vision, a flight of fancy, a collective work of art.

How was this imaginary Canada conceived and how has it evolved? Where and how can it be seen? What is it worth? What does it mean? What is the relationship of this private mental image of Canada to the physical, political nation-state—that huge, inert, wounded beaver, bellowing on the block, surrounded by butchers of all kinds honing their cleavers?

What are the strengths and weakness of this other, imaginary Canada? What are its good parts and its bad parts? Is it wearing well? Is it in need of restoration?

The Canada I am talking about is not a political football for politicians and journalists, but an existential fable, a poem, packed with personal questions for individuals to think about for themselves. Questions like, "What flag am I willing to die for?"—only less pompous, for it is a bit much to contemplate dying for a flag that is thirty years old. Better to keep it on the level of, "What sort of person do I see when I look in the mirror?" or, "What adjective do I wish to attach to myself when on vacation in Paris?"

North American? And we thought *Canada* was a vague concept!

Have you been to North America? Do we envisage a time when the tourist from Medicine Hat will proclaim to his Parisian counterpart: *"Bonjour!* I'm from North America!

Perhaps you have heard of North America, that area between Panama and Tuktoyaktuk—nebulous but we call it home. Drop over and see us; just head for the equator and turn right. Oh we're one big happy family up here, from Mississippi to Cape Breton, from Cancun to Thunder Bay.

The leaders of Hungary, Poland and East Germany thought they could accomplish that. They formed public policy under the banner of world socialism, just as the policies of our current leaders reflect the monetarist mystics of the marketplace. Marxists too believed that progress meant that national borders would fade away, that a new "socialist" man would be born: "Good to meet you! I'm from the human race!"

While eager social engineers pored over their ideological mapmaking, the people who lived in these so-called "people's republics" seethed with ethnic and cultural resentment, nursing an assortment of festering blood feuds that promise to extend well into the next century.

Poles and Hungarians knew that world socialism was nothing but colonialism by another name; that, as defined in post-War Eastern Europe, "socialism" meant "Russian." The political disintegration we witnessed in Europe in the late 1980s was not the defeat of socialism as Margaret Thatcher and the Fraser Institute would have us believe, but the decline of the Soviet Empire as designed by Joseph Stalin.

That is the fate of all economic and social theories: They become the cultural weapons of empire. If Canadian business and political leaders, with multinational corporate directorships and accumulations of Aeroplan points, predict that our national borders will fade with the dawning of "continentalization," it is because they see a personal advantage in being absorbed by the bigger amoeba.

Lesser Canadians are less enthusiastic about the coming enlightenment because we know it will never include us; more important, it will never satisfy us. Questions about our evolving identity as North Americans—or citizens of the solar system for that matter—may apply to some distant generation, but for us, our children and our children's children, "here" is Canada. We may not have chosen it, we may not even like it much, but we cannot change it.

The obvious alternative, touted by our political and corporate betters, is to consider ourselves to be non-voting citizens of the United States: not unlike Hawaii, before it was finally put out of its misery and granted statehood after generations of disenfranchisement. While annexation as a junior partner of the United States may not be an enviable fate in many ways, it *is* an alternative for a deformed nation-state on the run.

In the imaginary Canada however, the one we hold in our minds, no such alternative presents itself to the imaginary Canadian. Although we may disguise what we are, our identity is not subject to will power. What we feel ourselves to be inside cannot be changed by legislation, nor does it collapse without support from government. The imaginary Canada will continue to grow like a weed, through cracks in the cement if need be, for centuries to come, whether leaders fertilize it or not.

In the event of a "sovereign" Quebec, things may turn out differently—but probably not. What does "sovereignty" mean in the late twentieth century, especially when inspired and nourished, not by the cultural and ethnic vision of a René Lévesque, but by multinational mergers and hydro power deals with New York? What will the term "Quebecois" mean when current demographic patterns have had their way, when the newly independent Quebec government is led by, say, a Haitian, and Quebec has joined her Canadian and Mexican cousins around the North American maypole, dancing to the American tune?

See you in New York, Lucien.

To me, all this is nothing more than designer colonialism—another way to shed responsibility for our imaginative and cultural landscape by ignoring it or disguising it, in return for the right to participate in the North American marketplace as junior achievers.

Not to worry. Despite the Faustian bargains of our leaders, Canadians are not going to fall for that one. Our flag may only be thirty years old, but *we* were not born yesterday.

The Best Laid Plans

We assume that the decline of the Canadian nation-state necessitates our eventual disappearance as a culture, when this may not be what is in store for us at all. Perhaps the imaginative Canadian presence on the continent has only begun to make its mark. As we have discovered in past decades, history has a knack for surprise endings, and cultures can veer in unexpected directions. What if the North American threat is not *to* Canada, but *from* Canada?

Of course, such a suggestion is bound to evoke snorts of disbelief, but the prospect of a transnational, aggressive Canadiana independent of national politics may not be as absurd as it seems—in fact it may be happening now. Perhaps we have more power than we think, or want.

As the physical borders protecting a nation's political sovereignty fade, its citizens' corresponding spiritual need for self-definition intensifies. After all, a shared history does not simply evaporate; indeed, one might suggest that a country's cultural strength exists in inverse proportion to its political strength.

How else are we to explain the resilience of Quebecois culture in past decades, despite the fact that, as Gilles Vigneault sang, "My country is not a country, it's the winter"? By contrast, is the new Quebec, led confidently by the Bloc Québécois down the highway to nationhood, to be represented by a Celine Dion, singing a Walt Disney theme in English at the Academy Awards?

How do we explain the current healthy growth of Canadian literature, music and art, the sprouting of Canadian studies departments in universities all over the world, and the germ-like persistence of Canadian films—with no screens to show them on—over the past decade, presided over by a federal government that simply *loathed* the arts?

Possibly, as the Canadian nation-state approaches its political nadir and confederation threatens to devolve into a loose collection of perpetually squabbling jurisdictions, the imaginary Canada will not only survive but experience unprecedented growth, will worm its way into the North American consciousness like a computer virus—all the more powerful because it is impossible to track to a specific government department.

As a "dominion" of the British Empire, we have been conditioned to live "here" in body and "there" in mind for centuries, yet this traditional assumption could reverse dramatically should Canadians, set adrift in North America by their leaders, cling to an inner concept of "here" as to a lifebuoy on the surface of a vague, unfathomable North America.

Well, it worked for the Jews.

Will North America one day find its cultural media infiltrated by a collective northern vision with left-of-centre views? Will traditional Canadian concepts of peace, order and good government begin to taint the American ethic of heroic individualism? Don't laugh: It could happen. Should their crime rate continue and their cities deteriorate at the current rate, as the USA paradoxically adopts the control mechanisms of a police state in their defence of individual freedoms, the *idea* of Canada could begin to look rather attractive.

There may come a time in free-trading North America when the cultural shoe is on the left foot, and the threat is us.

In fact, sometimes I think this has already happened. Why else would American politicians and lobbyists have expended so much energy—and lies—denouncing "the Canadian-style health care system," if they did not sense the blade of a very large cultural wedge, insinuating itself into American life?

Dreamland

For the itinerant worker in what has become known as the "cultural industries" (an absurd bureaucratic attempt to legitimize art to people with no interest in it), it is fashionable to believe that art transcends geographical definition and national borders, the only meaningful distinctions being between "good" and "bad," "classic" and "pop." This device conveniently evades the fact that art in Canada does not divide in that way at all, but represents either culture from "here" or culture from "there"—"here" meaning Canada as experienced and imagined by its citizens, and "there" meaning whatever imperial power we happen to be sucking up to at the time.

The distinction between "here" and "there" is rendered more ambiguous by the fact that our cultural and political institutions themselves did not come from "here," but were modelled after imperial institutions from "there," like Dinky Toys, in order to strengthen Canadians' identification with Britain against a looming American threat. Even a 1950s "nationalist" such as George Grant lamented, in *Lament for a Nation*, not the loss of an indigenous Canadian sensibility, but the loss of British cultural hegemony in a national "realignment" with the United States.

Like all colonized people, Canadians are masters of disguise. To get ahead in the world we have learned how to imitate Bwana, how to convince others and even ourselves that, although our bodies may be "here," in some fundamental way we really belong "there." Traditionally, our long-term cultural effort has gone into focusing on "there" as the subject (wherever it happens to be), while pushing "here" into the indistinct background.

The recent immigrant to Canada will search in vain for external evidence of a Canadian sensibility, and will find Canadians reluctant even to discuss the topic. This is the source of what immigrants frequently note as a Canadian unwillingness to reveal our true inner feelings about who and where we are. We do not want to reveal this even to ourselves.

Canadians are into psychedelics in a big way.

I live in *British* Columbia, whose capital used to be New Westminster but is now Victoria. Our neighbour to the east is Alberta—named after a daughter of Queen Victoria who never visited the place in her life. Few municipalities in Canada lack a Queen, King and Duke Street. I come from Nova Scotia—meaning "New Scotland"—and was brought up in Truro—a Welsh word meaning "in the valley." Truro is near New Glasgow, and not far from cities named after Lord Halifax and Lord Amherst. Other prominent places in Canada are Regina, London and Windsor, and of course Confederation took place in a city named after Queen Charlotte, wife of George III, on an island named after Prince Edward.

These names are more than commemorative symbols. They represent a conscious effort to shape the future vision of Canada by compelling its citizens to invoke imperial figures on a daily basis. And for over a century, it worked.

Now it is starting to wear a bit thin.

If Canadians have been troubled by a chronic feeling of global ineffectuality of late, a sense that we are powerless to make a unique contribution to the world beyond the natural resources we never earned, I believe it is because we refuse to look beyond our synthetic political vision of the big red map. We do not recognize "here," let alone know what we are doing here. We grumble about the "Canadian identity" as though it were a missing cuff link, while in our hearts and minds we huddle in exile from a non-existent homeland, adrift in a chaotic void from which we escape as often as we can, usually into the electronic opium den for twenty to thirty hours per week.

So detailed and so convincing is our incognito position, it can leave the foreign visitor with the mistaken impression that there is no inner life to Canada at all, that we are a nation of sober chameleons—when in truth the imaginary country is alive, and vibrant, and well.

120

The Errant Canadian

When my father joined the air force in 1942, he left the village of Hopewell, where the family had resided for five generations, for Kingston, where he was stationed before his tour of duty overseas. There he met Marion MacLachlan, my mother-to-be, a fifth-generation Canadian from the village of Burritt's Rapids, Ontario, a pharmacologist doing research into Phosgene gas.

My grandfather on my father's side was a yardman with the Canadian National Railway who ran a small dairy farm and sang bass-baritone. My grandfather on my mother's side taught school, ran a small cheese factory and a small farm, and was legally blind thanks to glaucoma.

My mother and father corresponded throughout the War and upon his return they married. Nine months later I was born, and my father took his new family back home to Nova Scotia where they have lived ever since.

Much has been made of the experience of Vimy Ridge, in which Canadian soldiers discovered for the first time a legacy of common experience distinct from the mother country. In World War II, another milestone in the pan-Canadian heritage occurred through interprovincial sex—the intermarriage of service men and women from different regions, with the result that future generations possessed roots in more than one part of Canada.

I was brought up in Truro, a distribution centre of about twelve thousand people of Scottish, Acadian, Middle-Eastern and African descent. The Scots formed the defining cultural group following the Acadian expulsion, and made certain that the town reflected their world view and their cultural preferences in every possible way.

Ethnically, the town in those days was functionally segregated, with the black population living in varying degrees of impoverishment, in an area known disgracefully as "nigger island." (Nobody seems to know or want to know how this happened. Sinister, unverifiable rumours waft about, hinting at a mass expulsion involving white soldiers stationed in Debert.)

When I was young, Afro-Canadians were not hired to work in local stores, nor were they served in local barber shops. Likewise, although there was a Muslim cemetery outside town, citizens of Lebanese and Syrian descent were regarded as untrustworthy and subversive. The two Jewish families in town kept a discreet profile and prudently decorated Christmas trees in December.

Nor were Roman Catholics on completely solid ground. Their ornate symbolism and their ritual gestures on such occasions as Ash Wednesday were regarded as pagan fetishes by the Protestant majority. Even the Church of England was a bit much.

A typical Canadian town, and a natural extension of the village that preceded it.

I learned to play snooker in a pool parlour owned by a Lebanese named Howie Awad, from a Syrian named Junior who was in the furniture business. I followed young black acquaintances named Clyke and Paris on the CNR passenger train to Montreal, where I discovered Memphis R&B. In high school I worked as a salesclerk at a clothing store owned by a Jewish businessman who dressed immaculately in tailored suits, played the horses in Florida, and whose wistful, philanthropic wife drove a white convertible.

For a middle-class child from a rural family, raised on Protestant sermons decrying Sunday sports, whose social life consisted of school lineups and chaperoned dances, these minority cultures, however stereotypically defined in the town's limited ethnic vocabulary, glowed as distinct mental environments to which I repeatedly fled for a peek at the outside world.

By the time I finished high school, I no longer thought of myself as Canadian, if I ever had. The word produced in me a feeling of cultural shame, based on my complaints about Truro. I did not intend to freeze my life away in some backwater. I would go where the real money was made, where the fast cars came from, where people did not care what you wore or with whom you were seen, where life was lived to the full.

The most uncomfortable fact for a Canadian to accept is that where we are has everything to do with who we are. We just hate that.

So I dreamed. Although too timid to physically leave the country (other than the occasional trip to Boston to see the Red Sox), my psychic commitment to expatriation endured. Through careful entertainment choices I nourished within myself the feeling of secret superiority that characterizes the colonial aesthete, with his Dave Brubeck records, his mid-Atlantic vowels, and his encyclopedic command of the dates, places and minor players in early

Hollywood movies. Perhaps the commitment of brain cells to irrelevant foreign data constitutes a form of symbolic patriotism, proof of devotion to our "other" mother country in the absence of formal citizenship. It is no accident that the board game *Trivial Pursuit* was invented by Canadians.

I became yet another Canadian who belonged someplace else, that international place where worldly, well-dressed people ponder issues that are worth thinking about; where the business is big and the lunches are powerful; where *bon mots* are traded at a higher exchange rate than wherever it is you happen to be.

Although I had longed to become a writer since puberty, by the age of thirty I had failed to write a single original sentence or to compose a note of music—and no wonder. I had defined my entire inner experience in terms of "there" when, lo and behold, my body was still "here." (Although in fairness, other Canadians have managed to produce thoughts from "there" while sitting "here"—a Yogic contortion practised to perfection by television writers and arts journalists.)

If there is a psychic ache worse than to be separated from where you belong, it is not to know where that is. I was the wandering Canadian, mentally scouring the continent for that place where I fit in, longing to redefine myself in superior company, eager to catch the train in that direction.

Years later I began to understand the price of a ticket to that other place: You have to renounce your memories. You must pretend that part of you does not exist, even if you can feel it. This mental training works a bit like a lobotomy, leaving you pliant but ineffective—a state characterized by that unspecifically positive smile worn by Canadians who flourish in Hollywood, skilled technicians with the receptive potential of vacant lots.

So I drifted to Toronto. I assumed or hoped that I would one day find the courage to head for New York—a natural progression, like geese flying from swamp to swamp on their way south. And I might have followed them, had I not taken up with Theatre Passe Muraille, a company devoted to producing plays from here—meaning from Ontario.

Never mind that there was nothing French about Theatre Passe Muraille; never mind that they had interpreted the prudent, vaguely anal-retentive Ontario sensibility to include the whole of Canada—a kind of micro-colonialism practised with complacent sincerity by Ontario-based cultural institutions such as the CBC.

I would quibble about this later. The important thing was that suddenly the creative process was not quite so mysterious as it had seemed: You went into the society where you lived, found characters and stories, then reproduced them, shaped into a more or less structurally coherent form.

How simple. Not necessarily fun, nor easy, nor successful, but simple.

I finally had a concept of "here" I could work with—less restrictive than Truro, more definite than North America, and not the United States. A place I could view first-hand and replicate in a form other than something I saw in a movie. A place I could hold in my mind.

Lies My Father Told Me

Our flag is only thirty years old. I can never get over that. Nationally we managed to extend our infantile status as the "Dominion" of a parent country for nearly a century—an achievement made possible by steadfastly maintaining a number of false assumptions about who and where we are:

Canada is a "young" country.

Canada is nothing of the kind. The romantic nationalist movement of the 1860s saw the creation of a number of nation-states: Germany became a nation in 1871 under Bismark, while Italy was united—if that is the word—in 1870. Canada was formed in 1867. Unlike Canada, Italy and Germany do not think of themselves as "young" countries.

Canada lacks "history."

What we really mean is that Canada lacks *European* history. Though Native villages in BC have existed for five thousand years on the same site, we persist in the notion that, unless your landscape has "developed" (another loaded word) into European cities with streets and a town square, with libraries containing written accounts of wars involving European emperors, kings and nation-states, then you have no history. This is rather like pronouncing a cat an inferior dog because it fails to heel or fetch.

In the case of Native history I doubt if libraries would have helped; the government and the church would have burnt them to the ground long ago.

Canadians are a docile people.

We are not. We are a truculent, rather violent people, and know it—which is why we have tougher gun laws than the United States, a country that takes a more naïvely optimistic view of human individuality. Gun laws or not, I would far rather wander the streets of New York on a Saturday night than the streets of Stellarton, Nova Scotia. In both World Wars, Canadian soldiers were feared for their ruthlessness. In international tournaments, Canadian hockey players are regarded as skillful thugs.

Canadians are not a docile people, we are a *conquered* people—conquered from within, thanks to a long series of imperial moles, from Sir John A. MacDonald to the Rt. Hon. Brian Mulroney and Jean Chrétien, ostensibly working for this country but cultural-ly in the service of another.

For a country whose national historic symbol is a red-coated police officer, we are remarkably smug about our position in the democratic freedom sweepstakes (a kind of beauty contest western democracies like to hold from time to time). But if Canada is not a police state it is because we no longer need to be. We have men-tally trained ourselves to the point where the policeman is within ourselves as a part of our collective thought process—a mental dis-cipline that has made Canada the most successful colony in the history of the world, whose control systems are no longer imposed from without but arise from the centre of our being.

Pierre Trudeau failed to understand that it is one thing to repatriate the constitution and quite another to repatriate the imagi-nation; he would have done a far greater service to his country had he nationalized our movie theatres rather than our oil wells.

An empire, like a country, is nothing more than an agreed-upon concept, a habit of behavior, but such habits linger long after the mother country has ceased to be anybody's mother. Given our penchant for forelock-tugging, should we manage to transform ourselves into mental citizens of North America, the hemisphere, the world, the universe, it might not be a form of growth at all but an amputation, a reversion to infantile colonial habits.

When our leaders embrace Video North America, are they being cosmopolitan and "international," or are they natives in search of Bwana, a colony searching for Mom? Do free trade agreements proclaim our competitiveness in the world of manufacture and trade, or do they crystallize our subservience to the United States in the world of ideas and ideology?

In politics, business and popular culture we look to the US for self-definition, just as we once looked to the British Empire, afraid of what would happen if we started thinking for ourselves, terrified of what we might see if we looked at ourselves in the mirror.

Maybe we are afraid we would see nothing in the mirror, that we have been drawing sustenance from other cultures for so long we have become a race of polite vampires.

Like any small country on the fringe of an empire we contend with periodic assaults on the imaginary country from within—not because of any conscious action on the part of the superpower, but through our perception of our own best interest over the short term. In an unequal relationship it is not always economically or politically prudent for citizens to appear as themselves or even to recognize themselves. But sooner or later it becomes essential that they do so, if the individuals who make up that country are to retain any dignity.

For we are Canadians. This is a fact. We will never be free of that adjective.

Nobody is going to refer to us as North Americans, nor as Western Hemispherians nor as Citizens of the World, no matter how much we might want them to. "Canadian" is our adjective, and we had better take care of the concept if we do not want it to become an insulting racial stereotype.

For this can happen.

Watch the Adjectives

Scientists have no way of dealing with a society as an adjective: In fact, in a way the difference between science and art is the difference between a noun and an adjective. But God help the nouns when the adjectives go awry.

The word *American* can mean different things, depending on which South American country you happen to inhabit; the word *Russian* is a different adjective in the 1990s than it was in 1970s under Brezhnev, and different again from what it was in the 1980s under Andropov.

Adjectives that apply to non-superpowers usually depend upon how they relate to their larger neighbours. *Polish* has improved a good deal in past decades; *Balkan* has not done quite so well.

When unequal societies form an economic or political unit, the more powerful partner deals out the adjectives. The British, Dutch and Belgians applied adjectives to the people of India and Africa: primitive, incapable of self-government, stupid. Similarly, the United States applies adjectives to their Mexican neighbours: lazy, unsanitary, corrupt. And to their Canadian neighbours: dull.

And these adjectives have power—especially when they come at you year after year as you try to blend with a foreign sensibility. They become self-fulfilling. They get to you. They define how you feel about yourself as a person.

This is where the fate of Canada and my own fate converge: Canada is my inner escape from both the thought patterns I was trained to assume in a Nova Scotia village, and from my moth-like attraction to that great flame to the south. Canada to me is not a political concept but an imaginative and an existential one, with a life span extending far beyond the RCMP and the 49th Parallel and the Parliament Buildings and the twentieth century. Canada is my spiritual landscape, the space within the edges of my mind and the people who inhabit it. The space that allows me to think my own thoughts. To know my own name. To be here.

HOW TO MAKE THINGS WORSE:
A CANADIAN RECIPE FOR DECAY

Vital Signs

From canoe clubs to federal governments, all institutions decay, and for the same underlying reasons, but each in its own peculiar style. To reverse a decline it is not enough to detect it: One must identify and understand the culture that defines it.

The consequences of culture and style are not easy to accept for Canadians, who have trained themselves to think we have neither. Canadians traditionally view any expression of aesthetic interest as frivolous and vaguely effeminate. Trudeau excepted, the men who have led our nation look as though their hairstyles were left to them by their fathers and their clothes chosen by their wives—or, in the case of the denim shirt, their media consultants.

But style goes well beyond *couture, haute* or otherwise. For example, it underlies that bracing sense of self we feel on a cross-border shopping spree. Just a few miles from home, Canadians feel inescapably different among Americans, whose style is more demonstrably friendly *(Have a REAL nice day)*, confident *(This Bud's for you)*, and volatile *(Give me your fuckin' money)* than that of their Canadian customers.

Paradoxically, we enjoy shopping in the USA because it makes us feel more Canadian than we do at home. It has less to do with the price of Nike shoes than with our craving for a glimpse in the mirror, for a sense of our own style.

At home we are a forest of hyphens. I think of myself as Scottish-Canadian, although my family has lived in Canada for generations; drop that hyphen and the bulk of my cultural inheritance goes with it. French-Canadians too have their hyphens—the Parti Québécois wants to seize the hyphen and drop what is on either side. Aboriginal people negotiate *two* hyphens: one separating Canada from their status as Natives, the other designating their particular nation and language.

The hyphen jams its way in between our smaller and our larger selves as a reminder that none of us is *absolutely* Canadian. We all view ourselves in relative terms, plagued by comparisons with other cultures, which we inevitably see as more pedigreed and unhyphenated than our own. I can never feel as Scottish as the Scots, nor will a Quebecois become as French as the French; and who on earth can be as American as an American?

Some see the Canadian search for identity as an exercise similar to the philosophical substance dilemma: "I see the trombones and the trumpets, but I fail to see the band." The ongoing search for a core reality to a word that describes a relationship, and a shifting one at that, ensures that we will continue to ask ourselves "What is a Canadian?" until the glaciers melt, with no danger of ever finding the answer.

Ironically, by stewing over Canada with a capital "C," we overlook those odd, seemingly random characteristics which *are* Canadian—which inform and define our daily life and our institutions, creating a shifting collage of unconscious mental habits that, were we able to mouth the words without snickering, we might call *Canadian culture.*

Instead, we marginalize the subject as "Native dances," "Ukrainian weddings" and "highland games," and of course "The Arts"—a fey, European preoccupation which we support with our taxes because other countries do, and not to do so would make us look like hicks. (Members of the Reform Party are not afraid to look like hicks, though—in fact they seem to feel quite smug about it.)

But culture is more than the arts and the sweat lodge and the dragon dance and the perogy. It is the basis for the instinctive vision, that internal reflex that shapes our social transactions and the institutions that govern them, defining the style of their success and their failure.

Where do Ontarians come by that peculiar sucked intake of breath, lips slightly pursed—the immediate pained wince of caution that follows any proposal or inquiry, however trivial? What price does Canada pay for the fact that Ottawa, the capital of Canada, and Toronto, the hub of Canadian media, are also home to the sucked intake of breath?

And are there benefits to this trait as well as drawbacks? We are justly proud of our reputation as an "honest broker" and a "moderating influence." (How telling that the head of the United Church of Canada is called, of all things, a "moderator.") Is this also a function of the sucked intake of breath?

We agree that a major source of regional discontent is chronically poor communication skills, resulting in a legacy of misunderstanding between our founding cultures: How much of this is a matter of style?

Given that we swear by what we fear, what aspect of Ontario's failure to communicate with Quebec is illuminated by the fact that French-Canadians swear religiously, while English-Canadians swear scatologically and sexually? Similarly, when an Alberta employer, brought up to value eye contact as a sign of forthrightness, is approached for employment by a Native-Canadian, brought up to believe that to look a superior in the eye is an affront, how does that perceptive difference affect the employer's assessment and the Native-Canadian's job prospects?

These questions seem trivial compared to the federal deficit, but cultural weeds sink the deepest roots—those miscellaneous, unconscious tendencies and characteristics that grow without encouragement, whose colour and shape tell us more about what we are doing and why than all the hand-wringing editorials of Thompson and Southam and the eternal jabbering of our radio talk shows combined.

To Hell in a Hand Basket

A culture creates institutions to protect the existence of what it perceives to be order, against natural laws that work in the direction of what it perceives to be chaos. Thus, the police uphold the supremacy of the judicial system against the natural "law of the jungle," while hospitals combat the natural laws of disease and death. We experience these laws as hostile, however much we appreciate the wonders of nature, because they evoke a primal fear of chaos. All you have to do is be robbed, or contract a life-threatening illness, and you will agree.

But distinctions between order and chaos are not always clear-cut, and one can even be mistaken for the other. We are now paying a heavy environmental price for the fact that our ancestors viewed unmodified nature as chaos, something to be "tamed" with pesticides and aerosol deodorant.

Even assuming that we have established a consensus—that chaos, whatever it is, is a Bad Thing—what would we prefer in the way of *non-chaos*? What sort of order do we want, and how much of it can we take? In whom shall we invest the power to define and enforce that order? How much personal freedom is necessary, useful and possible?

Now we have strayed into unlit territory, groping for a consensus on what life should be like. Clearly no agreement will please everyone: from the onset, each plank in the structure will be placed with someone sincerely hauling in the other direction.

Yet despite all this, institutions get built. Despite misgiving and distrust and crossed signals, we create social structures through a consensus—*which is not really a consensus at all,* but the result of energetic arm-twisting by members of the dominant culture of the day, enforcing their peculiar belief as to what constitutes order and chaos.

This dominant culture, aware of its preeminent position and eager to impress its world view, forms the engine behind the creation of national institutions—in a style disliked by minority cultures as arbitrary, unfair and untrue.

Nothing could be more expressive of Canada's predominant founding culture than the Canadian Pacific Railway hotel. From Halifax to Victoria, these nineteenth-century structures dominate the urban landscape like supervisors in stone suits, decorated with the carved lions of Empire, colonial beavers and other allegorical depictions of authority and industry. We may have grown fond of these nostalgic monuments to the old virtues, but nobody suggests that their design reflects the cultures of the Chinese, Slavic and American navvies who built them; and their descendents can hardly be expected to mourn their destruction with the zeal of a Canadian named MacDonald or Laurier.

Although no institution is universally supported, some enjoy more consensus than others. We are shocked when HIV-tainted blood is administered by the Red Cross, or when family violence results in the death of a child; but however we may question the performance of these institutions, few will argue against the existence of blood donor clinics and the family, and we view their decline as a capitulation to a chaotic state.

However, though we may achieve consensus, it does not necessarily follow that our collective judgement is correct. In our struggle against perceived chaos we may tolerate institutions which are in fact consciously working for the other side.

We permit industries to coalesce into multinational corporations in order to defend the economic cost of our way of life. Extracting nourishment both domestically and globally, these corporations become primitive political units unto themselves, more powerful than many nations and prepared to destroy all challengers—including the society they were created to protect.

A traditional purpose of government amounts to subtle detective work, examining our complex web of institutions to determine which act on our behalf and which lead to chaos, with a view to maximizing the effectiveness of the first and minimizing the effectiveness of the second. But making these distinctions today may require skills and tools the Canadian government does not possess; indeed, the forces of chaos may come from within the government itself, creating political distortion (pandering to interest groups), outright corruption (friends in low places), and any number of variations on the theme of how to make things worse.

Take the current flap over the penal system. Scared shitless by American crime statistics and sensational domestic news coverage, fearing imminent chaos, the Canadian public demands that authorities get "tough on crime"—meaning "tough on criminals"—by imposing longer prison sentences.

The Canadian justice system, indeed our whole concept of "punishment" is the Biblical heritage of an ancient nomadic desert tribe, representing a single race who called themselves the Chosen People and who worshipped one God—a local storm deity—with one overriding purpose: the attainment of the Promised Land. For such a culture, when interpreting Jehovah's proscriptions on murder, theft or adultery, issues such as the criminal's psychological state, his previous record and the possibility of rehabilitation did not readily come to mind. The expedient approach was to stone the miscreant and to leave rehabilitation to the hereafter.

But for a secular, diverse confederation of races and cultures like Canada, things are not so simple. Sooner or later we encounter the alarming possibility that it may not be possible to get "tough on crime" and "tough on criminals" at the same time. It may be that, should our prisons operate with utter perfection as designed, they would *increase* crime, not decrease it—by creating an isolated, self-conscious subculture with the tenets and techniques of a criminal underclass, a veritable college of chaos.

Our government suspects this, yet lacks the power or the will to challenge its own traditional assumptions and those of its constituents—even if they are false. Lacking the imaginative tools with which to address and to communicate the issue, a secular twentieth-century democracy continues to pour millions each year into a system designed to serve the world view of a theocratic, wandering desert tribe in the Second Millennium BC.

Not exactly a recipe for success. Small wonder that workers in penal institutions share a culture of futility and assured long-term defeat, haunted by the suspicion that something is fundamentally *off*.

Yet, thanks to political petrification, concealed and protected by the cult of the professional, these institutions carry on their misplaced, antediluvian work, and the real damage may not be known for years.

The Birth of a Bureaucrat

However misplaced or malign its assumptions, every collective effort enjoys periods when its social objectives, realistic or not, unite with the personal, existential, inner objectives of its participants.

These periods of vitality are often inspired by a creative or charismatic leader. Under such a figure, sports teams, military combat units, unions and theatre companies focus intensely on a series of immediate goals within a limited time span. Other priorities are set aside for the sake of winning a game, taking a hill, gaining a wage settlement or killing them on opening night.

John Grierson, a messianic Scot, imbued the National Film Board with a sense of mission that temporarily overcame its inherent faults; Andrew Allen did the same for CBC radio; Pierre Trudeau, John Diefenbaker and Brian Mulroney performed similar feats for their political parties. Yet while these leaders may change the institution's direction somewhat, over the long term, as new leaders come and go, as one battle, game or campaign follows another with attendant rallying cries, sooner or later a long-term pattern appears.

Workers begin to see a Sisyphus-like cast to the effort as they roll one stone after the other up and down the hill. Cultivating a sense of immediate necessity begins to require conscious effort. To assure a standard of performance, new meaning is found in something called "professionalism"—the ability to produce a consistent performance, unaffected by personal taste or a lack of personal motivation.

Once one becomes a professional, the inner vision that inspired and sustained the effort in the first place now becomes a *threat*.

And a bureaucrat is born.

Once the cult of the professional develops there is no changing the cultural assumptions of an institution—whatever their accuracy, whether they foster order or chaos.

New members who join the organization, imbued with the inner zeal their seniors once felt in their early days, are regarded with a kind of testy tolerance: *You'll learn.*

Professionals pride themselves, not on the institution's outward objectives, but on the inherited structure and its ability to foster consistency. The maintenance of procedure becomes a preoccupation and an end.

Decision-making becomes a profession in itself, carried out by a superior, faintly hostile managerial class—hostile because of their intrinsically defensive position, as the gap widens between an ossified structure and the function it is called upon to perform in an evolving world. Increasingly, if only to keep its chin up, management finds itself having to play down disappointing results and to manufacture optimistic long-term forecasts.

Long before any decline is sensed by management, let alone acknowledged, workers on the front line squirm with frustration. Yet though it senses unhappiness below, management seldom admits to the cause, for to question assumptions evokes all over again the fear of chaos that begat the institution in the first place.

Lacking the will or the power to initiate change, the institutional framework, like a series of bad spinal discs, continues both to deteriorate and to petrify.

The cult of the professional meanwhile excludes creative or charismatic individuals who might otherwise reawaken the institution. In the 1950s, such a person was called an "idea man" or a "loose cannon"; in the 1990s he or she is seen as a "creative type"—a non-team player whose insights pose the threat of chaos because they tend to question first principles.

Thus, the founding culture, together with its assumptions, continues its presence as a rigid, dominant force long after its effectiveness has declined, and *long after its members have ceased to form the majority.*

As newcomers attempting to conform to their new setting, minorities are reluctant to point out basic faults in the predominant culture; by the time they become an integral part of the institution, they have been drawn into its assumptions and any capacity they might have had for initiating change has been neutralized.

So much for multiculturalism.

Canada's national institutions continue to follow mental pathways created by the dominant colonial culture of the mid-nineteenth century—Anglican and Scots Protestant in English Canada, and Catholic French and Irish in Quebec. These cultures, propped up by the brittle husks of past conviction, continue to dominate our institutions—not because their representatives have jealously guarded their ascendency (which they have), but because their cultural assumptions have so deeply rutted the path that *nobody even recognizes it as a path anymore.* It is simply normal; the way things are.

The long-term effect of a blind adherence to established pathways is to repeat the institution's successes and its failures over and over again—which would seem to produce a stable system were it not for the fundamental rule of human entropy: *Repeated successes yield diminishing returns, while repeated failures bring about more and more serious consequences.*

136

In other words, if you consistently follow the same thought process, things will get worse. Experimentation risks failure; repetition guarantees it.

Thus, as time goes by it becomes more and more urgent that cultural assumptions be identified and questioned—otherwise, all we have to go by is blind precedent, dogged by the terrible suspicion that we may be discarding and preserving the wrong things, and that chaos is just around the corner.

Natural law, on the march.

The Decline of the American Empire

Entropy comes in a variety of styles. Yet, as with cross-border shopping, one style becomes apparent only when juxtaposed with another. The Hollywood film industry provides an example of decline in the American style; for the Canadian counterpart we look to the CBC.

The American film industry is based on an elegantly simple version of the American free market principle: Determine what the public wants, present it in an impressive manner, and the public will buy it.

Film companies rise on this basic foundation to become expensive yet fragile empires that naturally seek secure pathways to reduce the chaotic uncertainty of hit and flop. Having scored one hit, managers seek ways to repeat it, to use the lessons of one success as a bridge to another, rather than starting from scratch all over again. Similarly, having endured a failure, the company seeks to ensure that it will never happen again.

Should it score a hit, the company may produce a sequel—repeating popular characters and situations verbatim—or it may simply seek and encourage projects with the same set of vaguely-defined "elements." Thus, a successful film in which a child, inadvertently abandoned at home in Chicago, is threatened by a pair of comic villains, is followed by a film in which the same child is abandoned in New York and pursued by the same scoundrels; or the company may take a more subtle approach, developing films in which endearing, vulnerable people are placed in jeopardy by humourous adversaries.

Although subsequent films will seldom equal the original success, their reliability makes up for diminished returns—sufficiently to inspire a third, still smaller but certain success. The company may try to vary things, but without deviating from the pathway to success, repeating projects that do well and abandoning projects that fail as dead ends to be avoided.

In this way, the company seeks over the long term to achieve a stable balance of success and failure. A level of management evolves whose job it is to winnow out projects that do not meet the criteria defined by established success. Careers are built on the ability to define and to repeat the underlying pattern, the hit formula.

Individuals on the front lines of production respond appropriately. To avoid squandering months or years on a project doomed by its very subject to rejection (whether the current industry leper is the growing-up picture, the musical or the western), producers replicate the winnowing process of their superiors on a smaller scale, filtering out "unsalable" ideas and developing for presentation ideas that have won favour in the past.

Still lower on the food chain, writers follow suit with a mental screening process of their own, bringing to the producer—sometimes even to their own consciousness—only those ideas which they think likely to meet with approval.

Thus, the process narrows its focus until the day arrives when the corporate structure becomes capable of producing *only one show.*

And then the audience catches on.

Audiences want, however naïvely, to believe that somewhere there exists someone who is not trying to put something over on them: if not the President or the Pope, then let it be Clint Eastwood. At the very least, when they are manipulated at the movies they do not want to know it—and when they discover they have been had, resent it with a loathing compounded by the self-hatred of the fraud victim.

The illusion that the artist genuinely shares the audience's experience is an essential part of the act. The entire thrust of a film's pre-release publicity seeks to emphasize the personal stake of the star or the director in the theme of the movie, the personal traumas involved in its preparation. While in truth their participation may have been part of a several-picture deal manoeuvred by their agent in a package of "elements" assembled like an urban subdivision, the film must be seen by the potential audience as "more than just another film."

But there is a huge gamble involved. Should the public detect the manipulative contraption, an alarming sea-change occurs in which the audience's resentment of the current "trick" extends retroactively to similar films they once enjoyed; the same "elements" that once produced rapturous success, now that the unseen hand has been revealed, suddenly form a recipe for catastrophic failure. Once the audience has seen the machinery behind the magic, each repeated viewing of the trick brings on more fatigue, contempt and resentment—geometrically compounded, with interest.

Caught on the edge of a crumbling cliff, executives scramble for a new formula, only to discover to their horror that, structurally, they are only prepared to perform *one* trick—a dilemma Hollywood production companies share with other bloated, market-oriented industries capable of producing essentially one weapon, one car, or one TV talk show format.

Suddenly trade papers explode with firings, bankruptcies and substance-abuse counselling. Spectacular failure has become an American cultural archetype in itself, a stock plot in which yesterday's whiz kid becomes the dolt of the hour.

Decline in the American style.

In Canada, however, decay takes an entirely different style. We seldom design or own the machines that ensnare us: They were borrowed from somebody else, by somebody else, many years ago. In the Canadian style, the pathway to failure is usually pointed in a direction that was never right for us from the beginning, making it possible for a venerable Canadian institution to pass from inception to decay without pausing for success.

The CBC and Who

Born out of a colonial desire to protect our British heritage against perceived American cultural incursion, the Broadcasting Act of 1936 called for a national medium of public communication, a CPR for the twentieth century, an electronic railroad joining Canadians "from sea to sea."

Characteristically, in implementing the legislation, Canadian bureaucrats sought a beaten path to minimize personal responsibility should trouble arise—and what could be safer than to follow the lead of the mother country? So they turned, not to the CPR (which had already established a limited national radio network), but to the British Broadcasting Corporation: a government-sponsored, tax-funded cultural monolith designed to represent a tiny, overpopulated island characterized by a feudal class system, together with an assumed distinction between "high" and "low" culture.

The BBC structure, together with its cultural assumptions, was carefully transplanted (thanks to a range of British-trained managerial and technical personnel) into Canadian soil—to serve a huge, underpopulated country for which "high" and "low" culture represented, not the products of indigenous classes, but imported artifacts from Britain and the United States, respectively.

The CBC was thus structured, not as an indigenous voice, but as a garrison of one foreign culture against the subversive influence of another.

Whatever the intentions of the Broadcasting Act, the CBC followed the pathway of an elite, paternalistic medium with a built-in assumption that popular culture represented a capitulation to the Americans. The organization then went on to develop programs whose consistent underlying purpose was to edify and to educate "the masses."

From the outset, the CBC inspired resentment on all sides. Audiences resented having to listen to broadcasters—frequently with British accents—who always seemed to be talking down to them, while broadcasters felt bewildered and hurt by the cold reception that greeted their efforts to enlighten. Meanwhile, governments came to bitterly regret having created a national voice with the power to criticize government.

Yet, despite the stubborn ingratitude of the audience, the hostility of politicians and the contempt of the private enterprise sector, generations of CBC professionals marched forward, leaving a trail of bureaucrats in their wake to deepen the well-rutted trench.

Inappropriately centralized, at odds with the culture it served, doomed to long-term failure, the CBC dug into its deep pockets to buy and build a national radio presence, which in turn attracted brilliant "creative types," who in turn produced individual successes—programs which earned CBC Radio an "international recognition," despite a maddening lack of appreciation at home.

With the creation of CBC television, the stakes rose, for television was destined to become a far more potent cultural force than radio. Made up entirely of words and music, radio programs are literary, operatic vehicles, whereas television transmits moving pictures. Freed of the literary constraints of radio, television engages an audience on a sub-literary level—populist, immediate, flashy and, to cultural elitists at the CBC, as American as a rodeo.

Thus, in the 1950s the crown corporation was called upon to focus its resources on a medium whose cultural habitat it was created to fight. Is it any wonder that the CBC's move to TV was at best half-hearted and at worst downright self-destructive?

Still, any long-term, structural decline is bound to be brightened by isolated successes. Individual programs, from *Flight Into Danger* to *Anne of Green Gables* to *The Boys of St. Vincent* were seized year after year by management as evidence that their thankless work was about to bear late-in-the-season fruit. Ironically, the creators of these successes were simultaneously placed in quarantine as "creative types" lacking the consistency for long-term corporate success. Inevitably, they made their escape to the US, where they could produce popular TV without having to pull their lapels over their faces.

Undeterred by a steady drain of "creative types," the public broadcasting army marched on, professionals to the end, carrying on their morally superior work while "the masses" tuned in to the American networks. American pop culture lacked nourishment and fostered unhealthy attitudes; curiously, this only enhanced its appeal to Canadians as an escape from the cultural force-feeding that characterized patriarchal British institutions like the CBC.

Fingerpointing on the Titanic

There are periods in the life of any deteriorating structure when the slope turns into a cliff. An alert management will protect its hide by blaming the sudden downturn as a root cause in itself.

Thus, CBC budget cutbacks starting in the 1970s continue to be blamed for current corporate woes—not the structural faults causing the public alienation that made such cutbacks politically feasible.

At a time when the network most requires a popular mandate to survive, the potential audience has become so conditioned by American TV that, to win even a respectable share, the CBC now has no choice but to imitate the Americans. Having failed to gather a loyal audience during its growth years by developing a truly indigenous style, having failed to become a cultural voice uniting the imaginary Canada, the CBC is reduced to an enervating game of monkey see, monkey do—a game at which it can neither catch up nor win.

While management tinkers with the schedule and sends out press releases about "repositioning for the 500 channel universe," the hole at its centre continues to yawn, bubbling with frustrated emotions that were apparent a half-century ago—and nothing fuels public contempt like a paternalistic institution trying to show that it is "in touch."

Of course, the CBC's intended mandate—to promote Canadian cultural unity, to resist the American magnet—was never more necessary and urgent than it is today, when it has never been less equipped to fulfill it. Indigenous culture was abandoned at the starting gate in the defence of British culture against the US. Structurally, Canada is not what the network is *about.*

To its public, CBC television remains a lightning rod for regional gripes, an emblem for that motto of Canadian self-loathing: "If you're so good, what are you doing here?"

In the face of a long-term institutional failure that can be per-ceived by anyone with a copy of *The Canadian Encyclopedia,* individual successes stand out sharply as bumps in the downward graph—and another motivational motor begins to hum. Individuals seek to stand out as exceptions to the rule who defy the trend. Thus, the overall decline of the institution becomes not a problem to be overcome but a context in which to shine, as short-term success is seen against, in fact depends upon, a background of long-term failure.

It is not that the professionals lose their will to reverse the decline: Individuals come to have an active *interest* in it.

Decline in the Canadian style.

Looking on the bright side, the CBC's salvation could lie in the fact that everybody knows. The question for public debate has now become, not "Do we need the CBC?" but "Do we want to communicate at all?" Despite its misplaced premise, the national broadcasting network is our principal cultural weapon in the on-going struggle against national disintegration and the threat of institutional chaos.

In fact, the CBC has become so tied to the culture of the nation that it may outlive it. Should the nation-state disappear altogether, the CBC could find itself a niche in the North American marketplace as Canadians, set adrift, lost in North America, reach for a shared vision of the culture of their ancestors, of the country they never did get to know.

The CBC and Me

You could have knocked me over with a feather when *The Journal* offered me a job in 1987.

Well, strictly speaking, it wasn't really a job. With CBC television, the office staff and management have the permanent jobs, while on-air and creative people sign temporary contracts. And my contract was as temporary as they come: one assignment at a time, on perpetual probation. But even that came as a welcome shock.

I had never worked for the CBC, although I had frequently been interviewed on TV and radio, and had done opinion pieces as a "voice" representing a body of current opinion—a kind of intellectual symptom. As well, two of my musicals had been bought by the network from independent producers as an extension or commemoration of their stage success. But I instinctively knew, or assumed, that I would always be a "guest" and never a "host." Whether too opinionated, too regional or too nationalist, I occupied one or another edge of the country, far from the mental construct and geographical centre where CBC people normally reside. Culturally, I was the wrong man for the corporation.

My invitation came from Mark Starowicz, the charismatic executive producer behind CBC Radio's flagship newsmagazine programs *Sunday Morning* and *As It Happens* and, since 1981, *The Journal* on TV. Patterned after elite print newsmagazines such as *The Economist*, these shows were designed to continue where the news left off, providing vivid analysis of current political, economic and cultural events.

143

The two radio shows represented huge investments for the network but, given the enormous cost of producing television, *The Journal* was in another league. When a budget reaches a certain critical mass, the show is no longer produced *on* CBC: It *is* the CBC.

Like any good magazine editor, the executive producer knew that no newsmagazine is complete without opinion pieces and editorial cartoons. But this is not easy to accomplish on CBC television, which is supported by buckets of public money and therefore feels a greater obligation than print media or radio to "represent" the various interests of its audience, and not to overly criticize those interests, separately or collectively.

The CBC news department has traditionally responded to this challenge, not by mirroring this diversity as a piece-by-piece collage, but by functioning as an abstract emblem—like the maple leaf. On a nightly basis, CBC news seeks to lodge itself in a fictional national centre, as a video approximation of the country's missing identity— like a stand-in for a dignitary who has taken sick. Personified by charming hosts such as Peter Mansbridge, Knowlton Nash and Barbara Frum, CBC news and current affairs serves a mandate to betray no outlook of its own other than as ordinary-but-intelligent, detatched-yet-concerned, Representative Canadiana.

The Journal's design as a socially critical newsmagazine and its mandate as a national emblem came into direct conflict when it came to the existence of an opinion page—after all, you cannot have an opinion and not have one at the same time. Opinion vehicles were devised one after the other to negotiate this contradiction, then ultimately discarded because, one way or another, they did not fit the mandate.

Then in 1988, the controversy over bilateral free trade with the USA polarized the country around the coming federal election, arousing intense national sentiments about the nature and future of Canada. The fictional centre became untenable: How could a CBC television show that claimed to represent the country take a neutral position about the future existence of that country? (*Radio Canada* found itself in a similar tough spot during the 1980 Quebec referendum.)

Rather than alter *The Journal's* entire format, the expedient solution was to engage another emblem, one of attachment, not detachment: someone to represent Committed Canadiana. But the presence of a regular columnist, an Alan Fotheringham, let's say, could be misconstrued as representing the opinion of the show as a whole. What was called for in these turbulent times was a kind of editorial cartoonist or court jester—an admittedly opinionated person who would function as an entertainer to justify his unique position in the format.

That person was to be me.

I flew to *The Journal's* offices in Toronto—a stuffy, hive-like collection of desks and monitors in a brick building on Carleton Street, overcrowded with tense, exhausted people and functioning as a revolving flu epidemic throughout the winter months. There I was ushered into a glassed-in corner office where the executive producer held court—a handsome, troubled man with a style that combined Edward R. Murrow and Hamlet, Prince of Denmark.

I was given the job—or rather, I was given a single unspecified assignment, after which we set about to determine what the assignment should be.

Following a journeyman season as a reporter and host of the an arts segment called *Friday Night* (to my own eyes I looked about as appropriate to the task as Yassar Arafat), I was asked to write and perform a satirical song in the manner of Dinah Christie, the resident musical satirist on *This Hour Has Seven Days*, or *Sunday Morning's* Nancy White. I agreed to this, on two conditions: Since I was not a strong enough singer to perform effectively live-to-air, and given the emergence of MTV and MuchMusic, I would pre-record in a sound studio, then lip-sync the performance on videotape, the way a rock video is done. As well, I asked that the executive producer and his staff choose the topic on which I would then write and perform without interference. (My experience with *Friday Night* convinced me that I would never survive the normal process of submitting ideas for approval.)

Back in Vancouver we completed the video, which was about the coming federal election and the voters' distrust of the political process. We sent it to Toronto, where it was aired and the experiment evaluated. (Life at *The Journal* amounted to a continuous process of re-evaluation and soul-searching. The high seriousness and the self-importance of the Canadian media professional goes well beyond anything you might imagine.)

Among senior producers, opinion polarized as to whether I should appear on the program ever again. On one side stood the traditionalists, journalists who viewed me as a violation of the neutral centre; on the other side stood the editorial cartoon buffs who felt I should be included—if only for entertainment value in what tended to be a rather earnest forty minutes. The second, somewhat merrier group included the executive producer, with the result that I was given a second contract, this time concerning PCB contamination in Quebec. That video was followed by a satire in which the selling of the Free Trade Agreement was compared to the spiel of a televangelist.

For two seasons I led a charmed existence at *The Journal*. Week after week, I made videos on such topics as the signing of the free trade deal, drugs in sports, the photo-opportunity and trash TV. I wrote unmolested, recorded in a studio with talented help and the latest equipment, and taped on location with elite ENG crews, who were pleased both to be doing something creative and to be doing it someplace other than in Beirut.

The fact that I had three days to write, record and shoot each video made it a hectic business, but at the same time it freed me from my internal censor. Once I had an idea, there was nothing to do but to run with it; and, since every subject called for its own musical and visual approach, no *post mortem* was of any value. Should we produce a bad video (there were several), or should my performance cause me to wince with embarrassment (many still do), there was nothing to be done but to brass it out and begin another. At the Vancouver bureau, a certain what-the-Hell attitude prevailed.

Back in the hive on Carleton Street, there remained the dilemma of how to position me within the show's format. The first solution was to create a *Monty Python*esque animation announcing my arrival at the end of the show. After one season that device was dropped; instead I was introduced by a bemused Barbara Frum as an afterthought, as though I had somehow sneaked into the building by stealth. At one point we tried to link my videos thematically to a main documentary piece—a good idea without a chance of execution amid the chaotic, moment-to-moment process of gathering a specific "package" together. Week after week, "greens" (evaluation sheets) arrived in which staff members observed that I did not belong in the show at all.

Yet I remained.

Miraculously, I even survived telephone calls to the executive

146

producer from a CBC vice president, relaying expressions of displeasure from the Prime Minister's Office. This kind of political bullying seemed to bring out the Edward R. Murrow facet of the executive producer's character, and may actually have attenuated my tenure.

Then came the CBC cutbacks at the end of 1990.

Back on Carleton Street, producers were fired and projects dropped—with fewer assigned to the "regional bureaus"—and I could sense that my days were numbered. Like a machine grinding to a halt, my assignments came less frequently, then stopped altogether. Creative types are never fired by the CBC: The telephone simply ceases to ring.

But it certainly was fun while it lasted.

Months after what turned out to be my final assignment, I received a puzzled, apologetic call from the executive producer: "We couldn't afford to do as many videos, but we never intended them to stop altogether." I told him I had no complaints, which was true—in fact, for some reason I felt sorry for him. I had a sense that a process had been set in motion that was out of his control. The cutbacks had not changed the nature of *The Journal*, but had forced it to retract to within traditional CBC borders, as a neutral voice emanating from a fictional geographic and cultural centre of the country.

The executive producer may or may not have realized that a similar contraction was about to occur in the corporation as a whole. In succeeding weeks, indigenous voices were silenced as regional broadcasting centres closed, series were cancelled and budgets slashed, according to a planned inward shift—to a colonial structure that predated *The Journal*. The effect of this shift was to push the executive producer himself—arguably a "creative type" among CBC management—to the margins of the corporation.

The tragic death of Barbara Frum provided management with its excuse to implement a decision that had already been made. *The Journal* was cancelled and its resources absorbed by the bigger amoeba—a highly centralized, rescheduled, yet-to-be-designed package of news and current affairs that would come to be known as *Prime Time News*, hosted by gender-balanced, white, theoretical representatives of neutral Canadiana.

Once again I live and work in Vancouver, at the literal and figurative edge of the country, the place I occupied when I received that telephone call from Toronto. As before, I write stage musicals and prose, and appear occasionally on the CBC to represent a sphere of opinion as a kind of intellectual symptom. As before, I am culturally wrong for the corporation.

So, apparently, is the former executive producer of *The Journal*. The last time I talked to him, he was on his way to New Guinea to make a documentary on orangutans.

NORTHERN ANXIETY:
THE DELICIOUS TASTE OF DREAD

The National Emotion

Anxious reflection is a Canadian cottage industry. No book list, spring or fall, would be complete without at least one exhaustive, humour-free malediction on what is wrong with the country, together with statistical and anecdotal proof (or no proof at all) that something terrible is poised to happen if Something Is Not Done.

In recent years, two major contributions to the genre appeared to conspicuous éclat. Mr. Gairdner's *The Trouble With Canada*, thunder from the right in a volume about as thick as a piece of steak, denounces our decadent morality, our coddling of criminals, our craven retreat from self-reliance and our fetish for bilingual labels on cereal boxes—let alone French toast. Meanwhile, from an entirely different, almost romantically liberal garrison marches *The Betrayal of Canada*: In fewer pages but with neat multi-coloured graphs, Mr. Hurtig aims the accusing finger at our declining sovereignty, our coddling of American multinationals, our craven capitulation to foreign ownership and our fetish for Reaganite accounting practices.

Both books enjoyed enormous sales, generating handsome royalties for their cheerless scribes.

Though emanating from opposite poles of the political spectrum, the two messages, stripped of specific complaints, carry eerily similar themes: There was a time when Canada was better, now it is getting worse, and things will be unbearable in the future if Something Is Not Done.

Both books conclude with various prescriptions for a cure, with varying plausibility and practicability, but most readers skim those parts, for the appeal of these books is in the spasms of anxiety they rouse in the reader prior to reaching these conclusions, the shiver of delicious dread Canadians enjoy so much. (Perhaps bookstores should stock these books, not under the rubric of "Politics" but in the "Horror" section, next to Stephen King novels.)

It is noble and normal to dislike the government of the day. Democracy is an imperfect instrument at best, and our form of it seems to have become a career niche for doggedly ambitious lawyers and businessmen with inferior *curriculum vitae*, chasing the table scraps of prestige and power. But our appetite for public deprecation is not sated with a contempt for politicians and their momentary regimes; we like to take it out on the nation as a whole.

Whenever we do not care for something about the country (which is almost always, it does not take much), in our very next breath we wonder whether any of it is worth the trouble, whether it would not be best if we simply gave Canada a final push off the cliff and saved ourselves the annoyance.

During the 1992 Winter Olympics, the Canadian skater Kurt Browning fell, and had to settle for fourth place. It did not signal the end of Browning's distinguished career, which would continue for several more years ("Career" seems hardly the word to describe a sport in which the stumble of a man in his twenties is as poignant and inevitable as the death of Picasso.) Nor was it the end of Canada's skating team: A mere two years later, starring Elvis Stoiko (the name itself is a work of dazzling showmanship), they would garner more medals than ever before.

In hindsight, how instructive it is to review coverage of the 1992 Browning tumble in *The Globe and Mail*, our self-styled "national newspaper," whose sports reporter was moved by the Browning calamity to sound the call for terminal handwringing (like duck calls, handwringers can be purchased at Toronto sports stores), describing the event as "putting an end to the pretence that Canada is a power in winter sports."

Oh, really? That bad, was it?

How very Canadian. We do not merely make a mistake, we do not simply lose at a skating event, we lay bare the illusion that we were ever any good at *anything*.

On what thin ice we tread, we Canadians—with not only our present and future unhappiness to fret about, but with the ever-present hazard that even our rare moments of past delight will be unmasked as a fraud.

Never mind. The important thing is to *worry*.

I have a theory, unsubstantiated as usual, that the emotionally overheated climate of nineteenth-century romantic nationalism left each nation-state blessed or cursed with its own dominant collective emotion—a specific feeling that was to become identified with the nation itself, entrenched in its history and philosophy and evoked by generations of writers and politicians in the attempt to capture an audience and to capitalize upon the national "mood."

Thus, Russia is soaked with unspecific nostalgia and regret, whether in the plays of Chekhov and Turgenev, the novels of Tolstoy and Pasternak, or the national pleading of Gorbachev, Yeltsin and Zhiranovsky.

Similarly, France bristles with aesthetic scorn—aggressive or defensive, while Germany aches with transcendent longing—raving or wounded; the United States swells with hope—dashed or not; and plucky Britain remains unspecifically chaste against a queue of real and imagined molesters.

As for Canada, we squirm with anxiety. We love anxiety. We crave it. We identify with it. We are addicted to it.

It could be the weather: Capricious and arbitrary as a marble Greek God, the weather defines a disproportionate slice of the Canadian life span; it often ruins our plans, whatever they may be; and there is absolutely nothing to be done about it, other than to get out of it as best we can.

Or perhaps the entrenchment of our common anxiety as the characteristically Canadian emotion arises from the fact that so much of our national consciousness was formed while fighting foreign wars, as young men disappeared, never to return or to return forever changed—a time when anxiety became a way of life for the folks back home.

In any case, while survival may well be the national preoccupation (especially if you are in Northern Ontario and you are Margaret Atwood), anxiety is our dominant emotion. We can never get enough of it.

And we will never have to go without. We never lack some new anxiety to chew on, always with a soupçon of unique flavour, just enough to prevent us from admitting to ourselves that we have tasted this dish before, many times.

Those who toil in the national media regard it as their sacred duty to administer a generous dose of anxiety to their fellow citizens on a regular basis. This saves writers and broadcasters a good deal of trouble, since it is always simpler to worry about the future than to comprehend the present, imposing less strain on the mind and the vocabulary. No new insight is required to conclude a piece in *MacLean's,* or an item on *The CTV National News,* with the standard open, anxious question: "The future is ominous: Does it contain disaster or calamity? That remains to be seen."

Our TV newscasters seem to have been chosen for a specific look of sympathy in the eyes, the one perfected by specialists in geriatric medicine—benevolent professionals "breaking" the news that a loved one is about to pass away.

Canadians snap at it like trout. One of the most privileged nations in the world, we treasure anxiety as an amulet, believing that, if we display enough worry about the future, God will forget to punish us for squandering our good fortune in the present.

We cling to anxiety even when it contradicts observable fact and experience—for after all, if there is one thing we should have noticed by now, it is that few predictions in the twentieth century have ever come true, and that few of the truly earth-shaking events have ever been accurately predicted. The reunification of Germany, the collapse of the Soviet Union, the outbreak of the Gulf War, the rise and fall and rebirth of Quebec separatism, the demolition of the Progressive Conservative party—none of these landmarks of the past decade were foreseen, despite an unlimited swarm of consultants, pollsters, columnists and TV pundits, collecting hearty stipends to gaze into their flow charts, crystal balls and the entrails of sheep.

In other words, there is probably no justification to *any* specific anxiety. None of it will come true. When we read or hear a catastrophic prediction there is every reason to assume that, should disaster occur, it will come from an entirely different direction.

Canadians are not swayed by this. By the time a popular anxiety proves false and futile, we are already staring at some new doomsday clock, ticking away. In the late 1970s we worried that world supplies of fossil fuels would run dry, that our cars would become backyard planters while we froze in the dark; in the early 1980s we worried that interest rates and real estate prices would rise to the point where families would be unable to own a home, or indeed to own anything at all.

Neither of these disasters came to pass, but we were not held back for a second. Hindsight makes past anxieties appear benign and cute, contributing to our sense that things are getting worse, to our nostalgia for a past that, from where we now stand, looks less fearful than our present position—even though we were worried sick at the time.

Thus, we take no comfort in the reduced risk of a nuclear holocaust: Instead, we remember the Cold War as an era that produced some great movies. In a world teeming with minor blood feuds and anonymous terrorists, we long for a simpler time when it was the Reds against the Free World. Things seem much more complicated now. What are we going to do? Where are we going?

At least we are not smug, we say—forgetting that it is both possible and very Canadian to be anxious and smug at the same time.

Diminishing Returns

However, so many new participants have crowded the Canadian anxiety sweepstakes, we may have reached saturation level.

Business leaders urge us to worry about our ability to compete with Louisiana, then Korea, then Mexico; whether our backs will break from the debt load unless workers lower their wage demands and governments lower safety and environmental standards to the level of a Third World sweatshop. Nightly door-to-door environmental fund raisers and suppertime telephone solicitors alert us to impending global collapse, unless the human race cooperates and sacrifices, to a degree historically unprecedented and genetically unlikely. Fundamentalist Christians, Moslems, and members of the Reform Party poke at us over the collapse of our moral value system (such as it is), and our need to turn back the clock—something that has never been done in history other than to switch to Daylight Saving Time. Like incompetent backseat drivers, opinion leaders point hysterically to the left and the right while vainly searching for a nonexistent reverse gear, grinding away.

Then in our spare time we can always worry about whether we will contract AIDS, or some other new and incurable disease (like the newly popular "flesh-eating" staph virus), and die waiting for a hospital bed; or whether our children will graduate from high school armed, drugged and illiterate; or whether we will be shot from a passing car while walking to Shoppers Drug Mart for a package of carcinogenic cigarettes.

Lately, there have been indications that Canadians may finally have begun to lose our taste for anxiety. We sense an element of self-interest in the high-pitched wails of the stress merchants. Is there no end to it? To be Canadian, do we have to spend every day of our lives *worrying*?

For this *The Globe and Mail* calls us apathetic.

When Canadians elected the Liberal Party with a landslide in 1993, was it because we had fallen for its hoary, threadbare promises about creating jobs? Or were we charmed by the tacit pledge of its homely, avuncular leader that he would get out of our faces, would not go out of his way to make us apprehensive?

English-Canadians seem even to have lost their enthusiasm for worrying about whether or not Quebec separates from Canada, having rejected a negotiated constitutional accord despite the doomsday threats of three national parties, two newspaper chains, a clutch of business leaders and two television networks. Go to Hell, the country seemed to say. All of you. Even Quebecers, supposedly the beneficiaries of the deal, said *non, merci.*

Canadians are in denial, scolded *The Globe and Mail*—in the weary tones parents reserve for petulant teenagers. Start worrying right now. You are going to be sorry.

Maybe so, maybe not. After all, compared to other countries— Cambodia and Rwanda, for example—we have little to fear. We are about to undergo peaceful democratic change. This is not a tribal blood feud. No matter what Preston Manning or Lucien Bouchard say, we are not prepared to chop one another to pieces with machetes, nor will we lob mortars into public school yards. Nor would the so-called "breakup" of Canada, should it occur, merit tragic status. Tragedy occurs when a great enterprise fails and people are killed, not when an unwieldy piece of real estate is subdivided, nor when alterations are made to a suit that is too large.

Have Canadians finally discarded the hair shirt and worry beads? If so, we have one man to thank for our emancipation: the Rt. Hon. Brian Mulroney.

How splendidly ironic. You have to love it.

Here is what happened. Following the election of 1984, the federal Progressive Conservative government (remember them?) under Mr. Mulroney determined that its best hope for long-term incumbency lay in two related policy initiatives: a continental trade deal, and an end to the ongoing flap about our repatriated constitution.

The purpose of the trade deal was to effect a permanent rightward shift in a country with traditionally liberal-left assumptions, by imposing externally-applied limits on our freedom as a sovereign nation to intervene in the economy by means of tariffs, subsidies, and through nationalist measures such as the National Energy Program.

Tying the federal government's hands in this manner was an audacious move and not without risk, for it unravelled forever the geographically artificial east-west trading pattern that pasted this improbable country together since the building of the CPR. Having unleashed centrifugal economic forces long held in check by direct government intervention, the Progressive Conservatives then set out to achieve a constitutional accord, to guarantee that at least the outward structure of confederation remained stable, even as its ideological underpinnings collapsed.

The hoped-for payoff was a country content to exist as a decentralized adjunct to the US economy, presided over by a long, unbroken reign of monetarist Tory governments keeping, if not balancing, the books. Mr. Mulroney's party thus sought to duplicate a feat the Liberals had accomplished under Laurier, MacKenzie-King and Trudeau: to recreate the country in a party's image, and thus to establish it as the natural party to govern.

However, problems arose in the execution of both manoeuvres. As the ex-president of the Iron Ore Company of Canada, a subsidiary of an American multinational, the Prime Minister was predisposed to treat the trade deal from the perspective of a branch plant, with a tacit assumption of subservience—an understandable predisposition supported by economies of scale, and by the cultural relationship between the two countries as it has evolved since World War II.

Moreover, as a trained labour lawyer, Mulroney was predisposed to view constitutional discussions with the provinces as a multilateral labour-management negotiation, a bit like a marathon wrestling match: a series of *quid pro quo* "rounds" in which the reigning champ negotiates the self-interest of each participant, pinning each opponent down one by one with much arm-twisting, sweating under the pressure of time and publicity until a final grand victory is achieved.

Following this scenario, after a period of sabre-rattling and name-calling amplified by the complicit media, the Prime Minister locked our ten premiers into a room with no advisors, no food and no sleep. (Perhaps catheter tubes were inserted; the room was notably void of women.) There the combatants pummeled each other until finally they staggered out of the room, blinking like badgers in the electric sun, waving a document called the Meech Lake Accord and declaring a "win-win situation."

Not exactly a quest for truth, but let's not quibble.

Had this in fact *been* a labour negotiation, that would have been the end of it. But unfortunately for the champ, it was the constitution of a nation they were fighting over, not a two-year wages, hours and benefits package. Outside that locked door stood any number of parties affected by the deal who did not feel represented in the arena, whose leaders saw no advantage in embracing an outcome which failed to include them, championed by a government whose approval rating trailed that of the East German Communist Party at the time.

Removed from that locked, airless room and exposed to the real world, the Meech Lake Accord began to disintegrate like parchment.

Of course the Conservatives failed to see it that way, and their complicit media followed suit. No political party is prepared to admit that a failure belongs to itself and not to the country as a whole. Besides, nobody dared articulate the real significance of the accord: that, however phony and tenuous, it was the only adhesive that remained to bind confederation together once the trade agreement took effect.

The stage was set for an episode of coarse theatre worthy of the World Wrestling Federation, complete with flapping scenery, threadbare leotards and platefuls of ham.

Into the Kleig lights stepped our Prime Minister, glistening as though dipped in olive oil, puffy and grim—hardly the Ralph Lauren sportsman we saw fishing with the President in Kennebunkport. Behind him glided Senator Murray (so young for a Senator, such a brief resumé): thin-lipped and eyebrowless, like some prehistoric creature from the bottom of the sea.

They stood side by side, faces elaborately solemn, like forensic experts at the scene of a particularly ghastly murder. Senator Murray held up the cherished accord and pointed significantly to one inky scrawl—the smoking gun indicting the murderer from Newfoundland whose priceless victim could never be brought back to life.

All Clyde Wells' fault of course, aided and abetted by Elijah Harper. How improbable—a Newfoundland Premier and a Native backbencher, representing two chronically disadvantaged constituencies thousands of miles apart. Where did they find the power to scuttle an entire country? They must have had accomplices. Who were these scoundrels?

Everyone in Canada it seems, who disputed the deal or the process by which it came about. Millions of scoundrels, from one end of the country to the other.

Having read their hastily revised speeches, Mr. Mulroney and Mr. Murray strutted offstage, chins at an upward angle, like defiant French counts on their way to the guillotine. Away from the press conference scrambled our obedient anxiety merchants, scribbling away in a chorus of fingerpointing and handwringing. Cover stories in *MacLean's;* a full-edition of *The Journal,* with Terence McKenna narrating the doomsday scenario like a distressed chipmunk gnawing on a walnut. Reams of commentary materialized in bookstores as though by magic thanks to the miracle of desktop publishing, authored by anyone with the time to write them. An orgy of delicious anxiety, with the very existence of Canada in doubt.

The people of Canada remained eerily composed. They did not cry out in pain.

Did they not know an award-winning performance when they saw one? Perhaps everyone was too busy watching American TV, which squandered no airtime—prime or otherwise—on these calamitous northern events. Or had Canadians simply moved on to more immediate worries—like the weather, or the price of Vancouver real estate, or the hole in the ozone layer? Perhaps the spruce budworm had caught their eye.

Or possibly they had finally grown weary of the old, insoluble Canadian questions: "Why are we here?" "What do we have in common?" "What does Quebec want?"

An Old Joke

St. Augustine, when asked, "What is time?" replied: "If you don't ask me, I know. But if you ask me, I haven't the faintest idea."

There are a number of other questions in that category—questions like, "What is love?" and "Who am I?" and "What is a nation?"

We have no trouble with such questions as long as nobody asks them; but when the question is put to us out loud, everything changes. The inarticulate nature of time, the self and the nation places their very existence in doubt. Our former tacit, working understanding of these abstractions seems invalid and pathetic. How could we have fooled ourselves for so long? How could we have believed that there is such a thing as time, the self, or the nation?

How did we ever convince ourselves that we were adept at winter sports?

We are no better off for this insight. It makes us feel miserable and lost. The absence of these abstract mental constructions undermines the abstraction that is our lives. We no longer have the means to communicate or to cooperate with each other. It comes as small consolation that we can feel superior to those naïve souls who insist on behaving as though time, the self and the nation actually do exist.

> Man #1: *My uncle thinks he is a chicken.*
> Man #2: *That's terrible! Why don't you send him to a psychiatrist?*
> Man #1: *Because we need the eggs.*

Although we like to worry, English-Canadians have no patience for philosophical Gordian knots. We are not existentialists. We are a northern, practical people, with little patience for anything that cannot be hit with an axe, dug with a shovel or hauled about in pails. Unlike the substance dilemma, the northern cold is extremely tangible; if you deny its reality, you will pay. Squirrels who daydream about the nature of squirrelness when they could be stocking up for winter, will starve, freeze or, worst of all, mooch off their fellow squirrels.

However, just because we like to worry about something, it does not follow that we want to spend time thinking about it. We do not take pleasure in life's insoluble mysteries. We do not ask, "What is time?" We buy watches, and worry about being "on time" more than other cultures do.

By the same token, just because we worry about Canada's future, it does not follow that we want to talk about the constitution. While it may be a topic for occasional letters to the editor, most of us are content to leave the constitution under lock and key—where it would still be, were it not for Pierre Trudeau who, in his well-heeled idle youth, read far too much Balzac for his own good.

French-Canadians, unlike their English-Canadian counterparts, dearly love to wrangle over time and the self and nationhood. *Le Devoir* is full of that sort of thing. Quebecers spend afternoons at it, over their Pernods and gin fizzes, munching plates of poutine. Ontarians in Cornwall, just across the border, want none of it. They hate that sort of discussion, and resent people who bring it up— especially when they do so in French.

In this context, we can see the problem with the Meech Lake Accord, the Charlottetown Accord, and other attempts to reach constitutional harmony. Simply bringing up the subject put English-Canadians in a cranky mood that had nothing whatever to do with Bill 101. We did not want to talk about the constitution, much less negotiate the damned thing, and the domination of the subject over more immediate concerns (like Great Lakes pollution and NHL expansion) made us bristle with resentment and anger, darkly muttering about such-and-such (it hardly mattered what) being shoved down our narrow, queasy, long-suffering, English-Canadian throats.

But Canada's so-called constitutional crisis would have occurred sooner or later, with or without the Meech Lake Accord or any other Accord—even had the document remained locked in a Westminster file cabinet until the end of time.

Whether or not we admit to its existence, it is not possible to ignore time forever, nor can we ignore conflicts within the imaginary country. Eventually these things demand our attention, and we are shocked to discover that, while they may be abstract works of the human imagination, time, the self and the nation are necessary, powerful—and real.

Often we discover the reality of something only when we see it slipping away: as when we become old and sick, having postponed a number of things we planned to do in life; or when the forgotten self bursts through in fits of rage or depression and our physician recommends alcoholic counselling; or when institutions like Medicare begin to shatter like Humpty Dumpty and vague national anxieties take on tangible form. We begin to doubt ourselves; it begins to look as though we can't deliver the mail, can't operate a railroad, can't treat the sick, can't run a school, can't make a movie and can't govern a country. Our funeral parlours, on the other hand, are second to none.

Canada is not in a constitutional crisis: We are having a nervous breakdown. And Valium will not help.

Anxiety and Hope

Like all deeply neurotic people in crisis, we employ elaborate mental strategies to avoid facing the problem. One of them is to adopt an attitude of sour grapes: The country may be more real than we previously supposed, but that does not mean we cannot do without it. Perhaps it is for the best that we break up, we tell ourselves, without asking what "breaking up" really entails.

For when it comes to nations, breaking up is hard to do.

First we have to agree to break up. Then we have to agree on how and when and where to negotiate the terms of the separation, how many sides are to be represented, who is to represent them, who is to physically sit at the negotiating table, and how the results are to be ratified by the population as a whole.

Only when we have made these agreements will we be prepared to begin negotiations—which will go on for years. For each agreement that in a distant, far simpler time, formed a part of the collective framework called Canada, a corresponding agreement must be made to dissolve it. Not only must we agree on the division of land, resources and debt: We have to agree on the areas of public life in which we will continue to cooperate. After all, it is not as though we can take a giant saw, slice up the nation, wave good-bye and sail off in different directions.

The Meech Lake Accord was a piece of cake compared to the challenges we face trying to dissolve Confederation.

Meanwhile, there will be no such thing as economic or social progress. Even if we do one day succeed in turning the country into an archipelago of proud little fiefdoms, by that time world events will have long since passed us by—and to our utter mortification, other nations will still call us Canada! The rest of the world has enough trouble focusing on us as it is, let alone as the United Designer Nationettes. Out of sheer mental laziness, the world will always refer to the upper part of North America as, Heaven help us, "Canada."

And what are we to do with the memories? Paul Henderson scoring the winning goal against the Soviets. Trudeau sticking a rose in his teeth while Stanfield eats a banana. Donald Cross, staring white-faced at the camera. The school bus tour to Expo 67. Where will we put the war memorials?

The genie, though out of the bottle thanks to Mr. Mulroney, will remain hovering about for some time to come. Plenty of time for anxiety, and plenty to be anxious about.

Unless, as I believe it to be the case, Canadians have grown weary of northern anxiety; unless we have become open to the alternative or, rather, to the fact that we are a peculiar national phenomenon—an alternative to a reigning monetarist theology that would rather exploit the world than improve it.

After all, although it is a wonderful world, there *is* room for improvement.

As the greed-driven, downward spiral of "globalized" living conditions accelerates, as the world chokes on its pollution, fights its endless, exhausting little wars, writhes with poverty, disease and political unrest, it may become obvious, even to Canadians themselves, that north of the United States sits a haven of accommodation, of possibility for the human race.

Where there is anxiety, there is hope.

Fresh Hallucinations:
Getting Away from It All

Eclectic Lifestyle

At the centre of Tivoli Gardens sits an exotic *faux*-Chinese edifice, not unlike something you might find on your great-aunt's mantelpiece—an outdoor theatre whose curtain is a fan of immense peacock feathers. Not surprisingly, the structure is named the Peacock Theatre.

Performances at the Peacock Theatre usually feature Italian mime. Nearby structures evoke Moorish and Turkish architecture, with an oriental bazaar and a Russian switchback—which is a kind of roller coaster. To evoke Venice, a gondola glides gracefully over the dubious waters of the moat. Evening concerts feature Johnny Cash and The Beach Boys.

Tivoli Gardens is in Denmark—a fact commemorated by fifty Guardsmen, who pay daily tribute to the Queen there, and by regular performances of the waltzes of Hans Christian Lumbye, known as "the Johann Strauss of Denmark." Tivoli is the centrepiece of Danish culture, no kidding.

Tivoli is named after a place in Rome.

Perhaps everyone would be better off if we thought of Canada as one gigantic Tivoli Gardens: Victoria, BC pays tribute to the England of about 1890 (the Empress Hotel features the Bengal

Room, Sahib), while Kimberley, BC evokes a village in the Bavarian Alps. In the West Edmonton Mall you can surf on an artificial Hawaiian beach, or wander the *papier-mâché* streets of New Orleans. Visit Kitchener, Ontario and you're back in Bavaria. (Kitchener used to be called Berlin; the name lost some lustre during the war.) In Nova Scotia, sixth-generation Canadians toss the caber in kilts.

Quebecers have chosen a different approach to the theme park format: "Québécoisland" commemorates, not an existing place, but an imaginary land—a Francophone ethnic wonderland, purified of English contamination and preserved in a climate-controlled environment. A piece of *pur laine* crewelwork, framed and hung on the branch-plant office wall.

From Yellowknife to Sherbrooke, no Canadian is ever far from a pizza parlour or a tavern evoking the Parthenon, a London pub, a French bistro, a Colorado ranch, a Mexican fiesta. When choosing a restaurant, you don't know whether to consult the Yellow Pages or your travel agent.

A rich fantasy life can be an asset as long as the here and now gets equal time, but in Canada this never happens. We do not feel it necessary or pleasurable to imagine ourselves where and when we are. We do not, on our own, feel a desire to maintain a Hans Christian Lumbye alongside Johnny Cash and The Beach Boys. We have to be guilted into it by people like Pierre Berton and Peter C. Newman. We receive Canadiana like Vitamin K, suspecting it to be good for us but not certain how.

We should not be too hard on ourselves, for we come by our hallucinations honestly.

When I was performing in England, my father came to London for the first time since the War; how surprised and hurt he felt when he was made to stand in line to have his passport stamped, while the Germans passed right through. At Ypres and Dieppe, Canadians never imagined a European Economic Community. It would have been bad for morale.

Nevertheless, visit your local Canadian Legion and you'll find that "The White Cliffs of Dover" can still bring a tear to the eye.

I remember watching John F. Kennedy on television in 1962, around the time he said: "Ask not what your country can do for you, ask what you can do for your country." What a speechwriter he had! As a Canadian, how I longed to be able to do something for

America! We shall overcome! Make love, not war! Right on, Brother! Where did I think I was? What was I on?

Who Wants to Go to Ottawa

Most countries can point to a physical mecca for its culture, a place that, more or less, contains or embodies whatever its people celebrate in other people and themselves. The United States has Disneyland—temple of innocence, purged of sex, crime and litter; Britain has London's West End—stuffed with the spoils of Empire; France has the Louvre; the USSR has the Kremlin, with the pickled Lenin reposed in his cozy bed, not dead but sleeping.

Canada has no such place, despite the fortune our National Capital Commission spends yearly in the futile effort to make Ottawa an attractive place to visit. Instead, we experience the imaginary country, not in the National Gallery or the National Arts Centre, but as scattered microwaves shooting through space, bouncing off satellites, rebounding into Canadian ears thousands of miles apart. Our national symbol is not the beaver but the RCA Victor dog.

The vastness of our geography defies definition, and if a country cannot be defined geographically, what is it? For most Canadians, Canada exists as a series of vague aural impressions, waves in space carrying the sound of a train at night, or a crackling voice on the long-distance telephone, or Don Messer's violin, or Peter Gzowski's stammer. Despite all our pictures of Mounties and lobster traps and maples in fall, we don't see Canada, we *hear* it; and unlike visual images, heard things are experienced one at a time. In an aural Canada, no all-inclusive image is possible, other than as cacophony.

Not so in visual America. We experience the United States as a series of sharp pictures generated by movies, television, comic books, *People* Magazine, and paintings by Warhol, Rockwell and Remington. We *see* America as a Technicolor dream, an inclusive vision we can share.

Yet even this is changing. Thanks to such buzzword conceptual trends as "globalization," the "information highway" and the rise of the "multinational," the Technicolor American dream is becoming part of Canadian reality.

The eagle is landing. Now what?

What happens when a myth becomes reality? After all, the potency of myth depends in large measure upon the fact that it *is* myth. A dream and reality are, by definition, not the same thing. You have to *not* be there, in order to be "in" a dream.

What we are currently experiencing may well be a mirage in reverse: Instead of receding as we approach, the oasis becomes more and more concrete and hard-edged and *real*, with used condoms in the pool and bloodstains in the sand. After all, John Wayne is no longer simply the name of a revered star of Hollywood westerns; today, John Wayne is also John Wayne Gacey and John Wayne Bobbitt—a serial killer and a man whose wife severed his penis.

As we outwardly commit to becoming more and more like the United States, as our products become their products and their cultural products receive "national treatment," the United States is going to become less and less satisfactory as a dreamscape—as that seductive "other" to warm the long winter nights. More and more, *America* is going to become the here and now from which we have been trained for generations to flee.

When gun control becomes a Canadian issue and Ottawa is the scene of a drive-by shooting on Elgin Street, how do we escape? To what do we devote our collective hallucination, should the US become...us?

Let Us Go to Denmark

Why Denmark, you ask?

For one thing, would it not be nice if our next collective hallucination took as its subject a country we are in no danger of becoming? After all, beyond Tivoli Gardens, it's hard to imagine a country less like Canada than Denmark.

Tidy, compact Denmark—not sprawled over a tenth of the earth's surface but tucked away cozily in a wee corner of Europe, where no point of land rises more than 600 feet above the surrounding sea. Civilized Denmark, its landscape pruned with nail clippers, its homes furnished in tasteful teak, its apple-cheeked citizens paddling along in their canal boats, munching Havarti cheese on open-faced sandwiches. Happy Denmark, where it is possible to get through the day without feeling diminished by geography.

Modestly proud Denmark, whose history of conquest (Sweden, Iceland, Norway) provides masculine memories, vivid enough to stimulate their little muscles, yet distant enough to avoid guilt feelings. Danes fondly recall the primitive heartbeat, the horned helmet, the trusty broadsword in the hairy Danish fist—not like our sneaky little victories over the native people involving smallpox and land fraud. No sex appeal there.

Speaking of sex, in Denmark they don't feel guilty about that, either. Remember when we first discovered Denmark in the 1960s, as the home of "free love"? The term has a bitterly ironic taste in the year of the condom and the sexual harassment suit, but try to repress that prim, rueful chuckle. Cast your mind back to a time when we banned *Lady Chatterley's Lover* while the Danes cheerfully slavered over explicit erotica. Pornography failed to warp Danes the way it does Canadians, who find Margaret Laurence too risqué for the high school library and for whom deviance means taking an excessive interest in the ladies' foundation garments in the Eaton's catalogue.

One thing you can say about Canada's sexuality is that it is a long way to Denmark.

For your Dane, sex is not a dirty, furtive little habit, but a healthy pastime, like taking a sauna. While Canadian teenagers lose their virginity squirming in the back seats of Plymouths parked in the cemetery, young Danes grope lustily under crisp duvets, windows open to let in the fresh air, with their parents sipping hot chocolate down the hall.

You see? Already you are dreaming of Denmark.

Friends of Danish Culture

It is not just its sex life that would make Denmark an attractive and exotic Canadian fantasy; there is also its generous supply of that most coveted late twentieth-century quality: Attitude. The eclecticism of Tivole, unlike that of Canada, is not a symptom of insecurity and self-loathing but the opposite—for, when it comes to culture, the Danes know they have one.

Danes spend little time asking what it is to be Danish. There are few propaganda battles over Danish content on their movie screens and television sets. They need no Council of Danes to ensure that Denmark does not sell out its national heritage to Holland; no Friends of Danish Broadcasting to ensure that Danes can communicate with Danes.

Most of all, when it comes to Danish culture, you know where to look for it, in all its variety and self-contradiction: You go to Tivoli Gardens.

Tivoli Gardens was created in 1843, just outside the walls that surrounded Copenhagen. A lieutenant George Cartenson leased the land from Christian the Eighth, after impressing the king with the argument: "When the people are kept amused, they forget about their politics." Tivoli was to be "for the amusement of the people." It was that simple.

Was a Canadian arts institution ever created "for the amusement of the people"? I doubt it. In Canada, Americans amuse; Canadians worry.

In succeeding years the city spread around Tivoli until now the gardens occupy twenty-five acres in the centre of Copenhagen, next to the red-light district: a perpetual carnival of circus, mime, theatre, food, flowers and music, in settings as exotic as the Danish mind can imagine.

If only English-Canadian culture were located next to the red-light district! In Vancouver where I live, the principal cultural facility (called, naturally, the "Queen Elizabeth *Complex*") is located behind the post office and cross the street from what used to be the bus station: a vaguely left-wing, federally-supported activity, served by underpaid, transient people who take the bus.

And things are getting worse. There was a time when English-Canadians could lean on Quebec for some borrowed glamour, but no more. Quebec is a "distinct society" now. We are on our own in a badly unprepared state, with Vicki Gabereau for company and Robert Fulford for guidance.

How Bohemian, how dramatic, how charismatic is what remains of Canadian culture—where theatre subscribers choose between the Blue and the Pink season, where you have to buy blue and pink tickets before you can buy a drink, where patrons gripe about abstract paintings in the National Gallery, where readers meet for authors' breakfasts, and Lorna Crozier's vegetable poems are thought to be risqué?

Can you imagine a Tivoli in English Canada? I can: a converted hockey rink in Mississauga filled with booths in which artists can be observed filling out forms.

In 1886, the toast of Tivoli was a high-wire acrobat named Elvira Madigan, who fell in love with a Swedish baron, who left his wife and children for her; for their indiscretion, society drove them to double suicide. In all of popular Canadian mythology, among all our war heroes, explorers, timber barons and constitutional visionaries, is there a single person who died for love?

It is time to relocate spiritually—outside the stone walls of Protestant and Catholic propriety, somewhere near the red-light district, where every evening is an adventure and a risk, where application forms are not completed, where there are no boards of directors, where people die for love, where there is standing room only, and where there is no need to buy a blue or pink ticket to get a drink.

I have never been to Tivoli.

CONSUMER OPTIONS:
HOW TO MAKE THINGS WORK

The Gap

Perhaps it was my reclusive isolation as a writer from "The West," but I found it difficult to focus on the last federal election. Although I adjusted my set, reception was poor, and many questions went unanswered: How does Lucien Bouchard train his hair to drape over one eye, like Veronica Lake? On whose advice did Preston Manning buy designer frames for his glasses? Who put on the first denim shirt—Manning or Chrétien? Who applied Audrey McLaughlin's rouge and mascara—Frederico Fellini? Does Kim Campbell perform judo chops in normal conversation?

We so seldom see politicians in the flesh anymore, the clues required for judging their character are hard to come by. We have a gnawing sensation that we are being duped—that our leaders have disappeared, to be replaced by spies with plastic surgery like *The Manchurian Candidate*.

Like the performers themselves, the issues articulated by Campbell, Chrétien *et al.*, the measures they advocated for the country, from deficit reduction to job creation to yogic flying, had a mirage-like shimmer. It was as though the country they cajoled and hectored was itself on television, like an M.C. Escher country—twenty-six million mirrors facing one another in a darkened room—or a computer-generated virtual reality experience.

171

Suspicions deepened after repeated viewing of election coverage. Everything *seemed* real as long as you kept staring at the set, but one touch of the converter button and the Canada that had been conjured up so vividly gave way to an empty screen, a black hole where something may or may not have been before.

When you see an empty space and cannot remember what used to fill it, can you be certain that there was ever anything there at all? Or has the space revealed its true nature—that of a void?

Questions of being and non-being dominate the imaginary country. Yet, most shocking of all, none of our would-be leaders, with the exception of Lucien Bouchard (who seemed to have a hologram all his own to work with), saw fit to address what virtually every Canadian recognizes on a daily basis: the slow fade-out of Canada, as a collective social endeavour.

In the absence of any discussion of the very thing uppermost on the voter's mind, the debates on television seemed downright weird. It was like watching Richard III discuss everything *but* the hump. The longer the subject was omitted, the more impossible it became to ignore, until the viewer wanted to scream at the TV set: "Stop! The country is *disappearing*, can't you see that? What about the *hump?!*"

Put bluntly, the nation-state called Canada has become an empty shell of its former self. If you hold Canada to your ear, you can hear the ocean.

Ordinary Canadians recognize this, not as criticism, but as a given fact. If public opinion divides, it seems to be on whether or not the discontinuance of Canada is a good thing. When it comes to the prospect of Quebec's separation, the question seems to be whether or not there will be anything to separate *from.*

And there was ample evidence to support this view. The Canadian election of 1993 took place in a country whose primary social and political institutions—governments, churches, schools, hospitals, social programs, railways and airlines, cultural and broadcast institutions, you name it—resembled a fleet of sinking ships whose crews, unable to swim with the current, expend their remaining energy outfitting their personal life boats and preventing new ideas from getting on deck.

Naturally, the captains who brought us to this state were long gone by 1993, well out of harm's way, snug as bugs in their legal sinecures, corporate board rooms, Montreal mansions, and retirement condos in Florida and Palm Springs. Their subalterns, half-heartedly at the helm and at a loss as to where to turn, now perform a number of variations on a strategy we might call Synchronized Sinking: Ignore the rising waterline, blame it on the deficit, and allow the fleet to go under—gradually, in a controlled manner to minimize financial turbulence.

Given that the sinking would continue, in 1993 we were given four choices as to where to turn on our way down: Left, Right, Hard Right, and No Place In Particular. During the campaign, Right attacked the Hard Right as too radical, Hard Right attacked the Right as too soft, and everyone attacked the Left. This meant that No Place in Particular was attacked from both sides: from the Left as too far Right, and from the Right as too far Left.

The result? Right, Hard Right and Left discredited one another, while their conflicting critiques of No Place in Particular cancelled each other out. The forces (if that is the word) of No Place In Particular, under Jean "Steady as she go" Chrétien, won in a landslide.

And the sinking continues. It was never addressed once. It is tempting to conclude that, over the years, our ossified political superstructure has evolved into a separate managerial class, imbued with the cult of the professional, who view the current national malaise, not as a dilemma to be corrected, but as an opportunity to shine as the best of a bad lot.

But perhaps I am overly harsh.

A Vague Uneasiness

Generations of Canadian pundits have asked themselves whether Canada will exist in the twenty-first century. Perhaps it would be more useful to ask a slightly different question: Does Canada exist *now*, and if so, where?

Is Canada a real place? Or is it a hologram, a refraction of light hitting the retina like a rainbow or the aurora borealis—an appealing sight, serenaded by federal hymns to utopian generosity, with the pot of gold at the end of the rainbow, the pension cheque at the end of the line?

Is any of this *real*? Or is it just material for election rhetoric, grant applications and CRTC hearings? Perhaps the whole thing is a gigantic scam, like a pyramid scheme or a chain letter, amassing currency for clever people who get a piece of the action early on, yet doomed to ultimate collapse because, really, there is no product to sell.

I suppose one rudimentary way to determine whether or not something is real is to mentally remove it, and see if anything is missing. So I ask myself: Without the nation-state called Canada, in what way would the northern half of North America be different from the way it is now?

Without the federal government, would there be no hospitals and schools? No roads and power projects? No—a change of administration would not alter the fact that these are market-driven products enjoying huge demand. But who would pay for these things, if not Ottawa? Why the same people who pay for them now, of course—you and me. The consumer.

Would some foreign power march across the border the moment the Department of National Defence shut down? Doubtful: Is our level of foreign ownership and control not sufficient to make national defence irrelevant? If our resources require defending, why shouldn't their corporate owners pay for the troops?

Without the Department of Fisheries, would our fish stocks decline at a *faster* rate? Would our forests be cut *less* responsibly by MacMillan Bloedel and Scott Paper, without Ottawa to defend our natural heritage?

Without the federal Minister of Finance, would we have a *less* far-sighted and effective economic and industrial strategy? Would we be less at the mercy of foreign capital, continental trading blocs, unfair subsidies, and the geopolitical power plays of Machiavellian multinationals?

No, I think it is fair to say that, should Parliament padlock its doors next week and surrender its powers and responsibilities to the provincial governments, as long as we stayed clear of *McLean's, The Globe and Mail* and the CBC, it could well escape our notice.

This is not to say that life north of the 49th Parallel would be any better, but that it would not be much different—except perhaps in Saskatchewan, the Maritimes and Newfoundland. But even in traditional "have-not" regions, any change would be a difference of degree, not kind.

Without the federal government we would continue to maintain a resource-based economy, selling off the minerals, fish, and trees around us—while they last—to foreign-owned corporations for the price they wish to pay, and buying these resources back as manufactured goods, at the price they wish to charge. This is a trait we would continue to share with places like Nigeria and Paraguay. Similarly, our work force would continue to compete with Alabama and Mexico for wages and working conditions. And our farms would continue to go bankrupt, trying to match foreign grain subsidies.

But what about our distinctive national culture? What would happen to our beloved Canadian films, plays, books, music and objets d'art?

How would we survive spiritually without the distinctive Northern vision we all hold close to our hearts? Those delicate hot-house flowers so lovingly seeded by the Canada Council, Telefilm, the NFB, the CBC, fertilized with millions upon millions of federal dollars yearly, massaged and coaxed into life by enthusiastic, sensitive bureaucrats—what would we do without *them?*

Actually, more or less what we are doing now. Despite the enormous geography between us, despite enormous variety in our regional histories, climates and landscapes, the vast majority of Canadians would continue to enjoy the same popular cultural activities—activities that by and large have nothing whatever to do with Canada, or anyplace else for that matter.

On our car radios we would listen to the same fifty or so tunes on offer at any given time from American playlists, assembled by broadcast consultants and editors of *Billboard* magazine. We would view the same television and movies from Hollywood (a mythic centre located somewhere in the city of Los Angeles), and we would rent the same videos.

Without the nation-state, our newspapers would clip the same wireservices as before, and their arts and culture sections would contain the same celebrity gossip, in which employees of Sony and Viacom promote their cultural products—coincidentally, the same products promoted by expensive paid ads in that very same issue. In response, we would worship the same culture heroes—dead, alive, and, in the case of Elvis Presley, missing.

Without the nation-state, our children would continue to play Nintendo and Sega Genesis. They would eat hamburgers at McDonald's. They would wear their baseball caps on backwards—or forwards, depending upon the season.

Similarly, on the streets, schoolyards and morning radio shows from St. John's to Victoria, we would continue to use the same expressions and figures of speech: At this point in time, hey, what can I say? Hopefully at the end of the day we'll get a life, be special, get in touch—with family values, the business community, the ethnic community and the gay community, in a bottom-line defining moment.

Speaking of bottom-line defining moments, it would take a civil war, a natural disaster or some other photogenic catastrophe to persuade media cameras to focus on that very special question: Is Canada *real?*

Although this may seem like an article of faith akin to the Apostle's Creed, I think there *is* a real Canada—more real and durable than our crumbling nation-state. But you will not see it expressed in the sales pitches of the private media, nor in the reverent national fictions of the CBC. You have to peer around you through the lens of your own imagination to find Canada. You have to adjust your set.

The Unbearable Lightness of Being Canadian

If Canada has ceased to exert a vivid presence, if it has lost meaning, it is because too many of its citizens have given up on the personal search for meaning, substituting in its place a hologram—a world in which meaning itself has lost its meaning.

In the dream world we are encouraged to occupy by our public and private media, meaning is a drawback. Just as, to our monetarist economic institutions, a tree has value only when it is cut down and assigned a price, to our mainstream cultural media, value and universality are attained by erasing the peculiar characteristics of real places. Coke is it. It just feels right. The CBC and you.

Meanwhile, guided by many overlapping levels of government and their media advisors, our political system has been reduced to a collection of advertising slogans, which change yearly as legislators compete for the feel-good tax dollar. It is no accident that such a large portion of national revenue depends upon the "sin taxes"—alcohol, tobacco and gambling.

That is not to say we lack regional pride—in "Super, Natural British Columbia," in "Wild Rose Country" and in "Canada's Ocean

Playground." Notwithstanding the fact that our media appear virtually identical to one another, and to the media of Cincinnati, in each region we put great store in our distinctive way of life:

In BC we enjoy a "laid-back lifestyle," as we soak in our hot tubs amid the majesty of nature. Albertans, by contrast, are hearty, independent-minded, crusty people in Stetsons, sleeves rolled up to reveal forearms like the shanks of giant cattle.

In Newfoundland, life is "slower paced," making a virtue of unemployment, and in the Maritimes, everyone knows each other on a first name basis. Quebecers are more passionate than other people, and like to live life to the fullest. Ontario is of course safe yet exciting, worldly yet steeped in Canadiana, and its citizens do not litter.

And of course we are all polite.

These are stereotypes of course, but they're *our* stereotypes. Our public relations consultants made them up, we paid for them, and we had better like them.

The "Canada" logo, on the other hand, its elegant, white lettering against a black background, with a little red and white flag flying atop the stem of the "d," has become a brand name for an outdated, soon-to-be-discontinued product with a bilingual label. Canada no longer inspires positive feelings among consumer groups. Canada is no longer in demand. And the customer is always right.

And Now...This

However, despite all the marketing savvy money can buy, all is not well in the "free" cultural marketplace. Something is missing. And everybody knows it.

In every corner of the country, people voice alarm at the deterioration of their way of life, which they see becoming more violent, more shallow, more vulgar—and at the same time less interesting. Canadians not only lock our doors now: We install electronic alarms in our houses and our cars. Street gangs, car chases and drive-by shootings seem to have become a youth fashion statement from Halifax to Surrey. Major sports victories now culminate in an evening of Los Angeles-style riots and looting, with reverse-capped young louts roaring into the camera: "Rodney King, Maaan!"

In our rural communities, farms are ploughed up to sprout shopping malls on the outskirts of town, which syphon off local cash until main streets become discount slums. Historic buildings become fast-food outlets, Starbucks coffee bars, and tourist "shoppes" stocked with tea towels, T-shirts and commemorative crockery from Taiwan.

Like the interior of a Japanese car, or your local Burger King, each region of the country is becoming more and more convenient and generic and less and less like, for want of a better word, Canada.

We fret about this. We suspect something terrible is happening, but cannot quite put our finger on it. We do not know whom to blame or what to do. What we do know is that it makes us angry, so we vote Reform.

That makes us feel better for awhile. But that creepy, unspecific feeling returns. Something is missing.

Two Nations

Let us summarize the results of our little mental experiment, in which we put aside the existence of Canada and see what remains:

What we have is a five thousand mile-wide queue of underpopulated zones, far from global centres of power, who sell their resources to the same companies, respond to the same slogans and buy the same imported products—products whose brand names originate in those same centres of power. When their children wear baseball caps on backwards, our caps swivel accordingly. When their kitchen appliances change colour from avocado to wheat, so do ours.

Yet even with the best appliances money can buy, the citizens of these little northern duchies seethe with discontent. It seems that, while we were cross-border shopping, some valuable personal effects were lost; and something nasty slipped into the trunk to take their place. We suspect that our synthetic freedom of choice has become expensive in unexpected ways, contributing to a climate of violence, dishonesty, superficiality, banality and greed, from which *even our leaders* are not completely immune.

In other words, when we envisage the non-existence of Canada, what we see is a string of *little* Canadas, with the same stereotyped, dinky culture we complain about now, the same sense of drift and decay, the same fleet of sinking ships on which not even the rats can swim. Ten little tugboats (and two little boom boats) with no place to go.

With a slight difference: Whereas the nation-state formed a rather undigestible population with left-of-centre inclinations and expectations, what has replaced it now is a dozen bite-sized chunks of geography, just the thing for crude yet effective political units with hearty appetites for natural resources.

But the distinction is a subtle one. The difference between a disjointed northern archipelago and the present nation-state Canada is a matter of degree, not kind.

Should Ottawa padlock the Parliament Buildings tomorrow, what would gnaw at our vitals would be the mental image of another Canada, one that is not a natural phenomenon like a rainbow, nor a constitutional accord, nor a business deal, but a work of the collective imagination, created over many years by many different kinds of people; a communal work of art whose *raison d'être*, if you will excuse my French, is its ongoing search for meaning.

This is the Canada that counts. Ignore this central concern, ignore the meaning of meaning in the mental life of the imaginary nation, and nothing works, and nothing makes any sense, no matter how you divide up the real estate.

Curiously, in this era of self-conscious regionalism, despite near universal concern over what we might call our distinctive cultural landscape, our provincial cabinets play down the significance of culture, usually as an aspect of "recreation" and "tourism"— something to occupy visitors while their camping duds are in the laundromat. Ottawa, for its part, has placed culture under the somewhat ominous banner of a "Department of Canadian Heritage"—as though we are already a museum artifact, a phenomenon that exists in the past tense.

As the gap widens between our brittle nation-state and our mutating imaginary country, the various departments and institutions of government grow more and more distant from the cultural issues they were designed to address.

Our environment ministries do not discuss the fact that our belief system, originating in Athens and Jerusalem, holds that the earth is an object for human domination, and views unmodified nature as chaos. But does that not influence our treatment of the environment, and does it not have something to do with culture?

Similarly, it is difficult to see how a Ministry of Health and Social Services can ignore the fact that the primary causes of our physical misery—tobacco, alcohol, prescription and non-prescription drugs, car accidents, chronic tension and hamburgers—are cultural products, playing to a master-slave dualism in which the body serves the lie of the mind. When you drive your body like a car, is it any wonder if it breaks down?

Jobs, jobs, jobs cries our Prime Minister—in threes, like the Trinity—but without a word of distinction between meaningful jobs and service industry treadmills for the subsistence of miserable lives. Are we so fiercely in competition with Korea that personal fulfillment means nothing at all?

Everyone seems to be in a flap about the school system, but if our children are not able to read or add, if they know more Spielberg than Shakespeare, more about Disneyland than wherever they happen to live, does that not have something to do with culture?

Perhaps that is why leaders prefer to ignore the cultural environment, the virtual reality we inhabit and its relation to the inner life of citizens: It is so all-pervasive, insidious and hard to grasp.

Yet the medium for gathering and disseminating the culture we outwardly salute and inwardly detest every day has a shape as definite as a beer bottle: It is that box in every living room, connected to a smaller box, connected to a cable, tuned in to a satellite, connected to...what?

Brought to You By...

No panel on education or crime or the family is ever complete without mentioning the fact that our children spend more time watching TV than they do at school. It is a staple of school boards everywhere in defending themselves against charges of poor performance. It turns up in issues such as gun control, youth gangs, violence against women, illiteracy, consumerism, racism, and general moral decline.

We have no shortage of gripes about the medium; we can scarcely pick up a newspaper without some worried soul denouncing sex and violence and its effect on "the young people." But where do we see this effect discussed and explained? Who bothers to connect the structure of the television industry itself—as opposed to the content of specific shows—to its cultural causes and effects? To listen to the debate, all that is required is for TV programmers to accept a measure of self-censorship, to remove automatic weapons, predatory sex and other objectionable Americana from the mix, then everyone can watch their twenty or so hours of TV a week and all will be well.

It is as though we are afraid to look at the thing itself, to face the extent to which commercial broadcasting has restructured our nation-state, driving the imaginary country underground.

To confine one's concern about television to the content of individual programs leaves out of account the primary structural purpose of North American commercial media, which differs from of the media of other times and places: Their purpose is not to deliver cultural items to consumers, but *to deliver consumers to an advertiser.* In the television marketplace, the network is the supplier, the advertiser is the buyer, while the commodity to be bought and sold is not the program but the viewer—you, me and the kids.

In the 1950s, Canadian taxpayers built the most advanced and extensive communications network in the world, on the theory that communication would overcome colonial attitudes and geographical distance to create the world's first electronic country. The Canadian broadcasting and telecommunications system was conceived by government as a nervous system to bind the imaginary country to the nation-state.

And yet, now that television has emerged as the hands-down winner among cultural forces in North America, thanks to the guidance of the Federal Department of Communications, we no longer use television to communicate with each other. Instead, television has become a tool with which to identify, gather and indoctrinate customers for goods and services. Canadians do not watch TV: TV watches us.

This distortion of the medium's intended national function has had a devastating effect. To counter it by changing the programming would be like reforming the fishing industry by changing the bait.

To illustrate the cultural impact of commercial broadcasting in a country like Canada, let us imagine what would happen if we ran another communications system the way we run our television networks: What if we ran the *telephone system* that way?

Imagine a system in which, instead of the user paying a fee for telephone service, blocks of telephone time were sold to sponsors, entitling them to intervene on phone calls at intervals, in order to advertise a product.

People would learn very quickly not to try and carry on a substantive conversation with anyone. Who wants to talk to Mom about Aunt Agnes' illness, knowing that at any moment the man from Brystol-Myers might take the opportunity to sell a hemorrhoid remedy? Similarly, business discussions would be curtailed by a lack of privacy; and lovers would find the ads for perfumes and condoms inhibiting, to say the least.

Under a commercially-driven telephone system, so quickly would telephone conversation degenerate, the advertiser would find it necessary to induce conversations *artificially*—to entice people to his pitch by engaging sensational, sentimental, controversial and sexy conversationalists for consumers to talk to on the telephone. (The telephone would become a source of employment for local actors between engagements—no doubt secured by controversial "Canadian content" regulations.)

Callers would be introduced to a new, improved telephone experience: conversations with people they have never met, with whom they have nothing in common other than the product financing the medium.

Naturally, public concerns would develop over "phone content." Church groups would demand limits to the sexual and violent content of telephone conversation. Panels would convene to discuss the effect of telephone conversation on the perceived deterioration of family discussions. Statistics would prove that children spend more time talking to strangers on the telephone than to their parents, teachers and classmates.

Telephone conversation as we know it would of course no longer exist. Taking its place would be a *symbol* of conversation, much as TV "family programming" acts as a symbol of family life: an entertaining, nostalgic vision of an imagined time and place in which people actually talked to one another. The telephone would thus assume a powerful role in the continuing evolution of the imaginary country—a role in competition with real life, since it denies the importance and meaning of the caller's life, should he or she hang up the phone.

There would be complaints of course, letters to the editor. Sometimes you do not want to talk to a phone personality, you want to talk to Mom—even if she stutters. Pure sentimentalism, would come the response. People who telephone *want to be entertained*. And Canadian customers deserve the best phone entertainment the world has to offer.

Just because Canadians lack the talent for producing exciting conversation, it does not follow that the taxpayer should be required to subsidize mediocre telephone calls. Better leave telephoning to the people who can produce the best product in a free marketplace. If Canadians cannot compete, they should get off the phone.

This is of course an absurdist analogy, but it is more or less what has happened to the Canadian broadcasting system.

Even commercial-free radio is not immune. Structured as a bastion of imperial culture against encroaching Americanism, in the present mercantile environment public radio has to be constantly on its knees selling *itself*—to a public that associates public broadcasting with the sound of middle-aged voices with mid-Atlantic accents telling them to read Shakespeare. The very fact that public radio needs to be defended at all puts its necessity in question. Does the phone company feel the need to justify conversation? Is communication a "consumer option"?

That is what happens when you pretend that culture is a neutral commodity like a toaster, that there is such a thing as "pure entertainment" or "free TV." Such assumptions create a meaning vacuum that is filled by something that looks, sounds and symbolizes the thing it replaced, but which contains none of the original content, and exists for a completely different purpose.

The imaginary country is vulnerable to this erosion of meaning. Canadian culture has always been a vague concept embraced by impractical people, hard to grasp and vaguely epicene.

Not that culture is ignored abroad. Ethnic groups slaughter one another on a daily basis over it. At the last Republican presidential nominations, "cultural war" was declared against a "cultural elite" undermining America's "family values." Within Canada, or at least the nation-state of the moment, "cultural sovereignty" is a principal reason for the threatened separation of Quebec.

If culture is the cause of so many problems, why is so little attention paid to the topic among our overlapping government committees, our interminable tongue-flapping national and local current affairs shows, our ponderous reams of editorial copy?

Time for a joke: Why did the Canadian cross the road?
To avoid something he'd rather not deal with right now.

The Cultural Clear-Cut

In the town where I grew up stood a magnificent Victorian Railway station, made of locally-quarried stone. It presided over Inglis Street for over a century.

In the huge waiting room, with its marble echo and its mysterious passenger train smell—musty and clean at the same time—stood a photo vending machine where lovers took portraits for wallets and lockets, friendships were documented, where naughty photographs were sometimes taken, with an accomplice standing guard outside the closed curtain.

Nearby was another vending machine with a crank on the side and a large chrome arrow on the face, surrounded by the alphabet, punctuation and other characters. If you put ten cents in the slot, you could stamp your name and address into an aluminum disc, suitable as a key chain and for identifying luggage, with a crown on the hub of one side and a lucky horseshoe on the other. We regarded these discs as souvenirs, like the pennies we placed on the rail outside to be squashed by the Ocean Limited into amulet status and carried as charms.

I suppose the railway station, if it was a symbol, represented the town's vision of the imaginary Canada: local, yet able to evoke huge distances and faraway, magic places, expressing the town's sense of itself as on the go and worthy of serious consideration, bound to the rest of the country with heavy-duty equipment. Touch that rail and you touched British Columbia.

The railway station was torn down in the 1970s, replaced by a shopping centre and a depot that looks like an elongated motor home. Does anyone in Ottawa have any idea what the deterioration of the railway system has done to the national vision of virtually every small town in Canada?

As a monument to the founding culture, Truro's cultural minorities would have been justifiably less sentimental about that station; to them its loss was no doubt less tragic. But who's life was expressed or enhanced by the thing that replaced it? And if a town thinks so little of its historic landmarks, how is it to make a case against, say, littering, or vandalism, or the spray-painting of slogans on public buildings? While we are at it, if culture matters so little, why do people complain about that triple-X video shop on the corner?

One more architectural boast from Truro: On Duke Street stood one of the largest wood-frame "Carpenter Gothic" churches in Nova Scotia, built by ships' carpenters in the last century at a cost of $30,000, raised by a congregation of about 300. Shaped like a cross, it had flying buttresses and two steeples—one at least sixty feet high, the highest point on the town's silhouette.

Inside, the church was intricately beamed like a ship with curved wood throughout. Huge stained glass windows rose overhead, with smaller ones glowing like jewels beneath the rounded perimeter of the hardwood balcony. From a centre pew the building appeared far higher than it was wide. In a stiff October wind its joints creaked and groaned as though the congregation were passengers on the Ark.

St. Andrew's Church was torn down, and its square brick gym renovated as a replacement. As a heritage site it was not considered vital by the town or the province. $30,000 was evidently a good deal easier to raise among the farmers and shopkeepers of nineteenth-century Truro than it is today.

Here is the truly amazing thing: I have been home on many occasions, I have talked to dozens of people on the subject, and *not one will admit something is missing.*

Like the fundamental decline of Canada or Richard III's hump, the very fact that nobody talks about it makes it impossible to ignore. What about the *hump?*

They point out that repairs to the church would have incurred a heavy debt load, once the government refused to provide a grant; that without repairs it was a firetrap, a disaster waiting to occur. Similarly, the railway station was really too large for the town, once Via Rail had been "downsized."

Everything is as it should be, you see. Everything is fine. And when Uncle Roy went in for shock treatments, he was just feeling "down in the dumps."

Is this yet another example of the smiling Calvinism so prevalent in Canada, a "we can take it" optimism—Norman Vincent Peale with clenched teeth? Or are we simply insensitive people with a missing aesthetic chromosome?

Or, more ominously, is the source of this stubborn denial of the obvious a matter of sheer psychic survival? To admit to a sense of loss over the station and the church would be to open a yawning, painful chasm, a terrible void like the pain of an amputated limb that can never be relieved—because there is nothing there to fix.

As the Canadian culture hero Otis Redding once sang, you don't miss your water till your well runs dry.

A sense of loss is certainly not confined to a depressed economy—on the contrary, in "good" times it becomes an everyday urban experience:

You walk down the street where you live, where you have walked many times. Down the block you hear a clanking sound and the gunning of an engine. You head for the sound and discover a Hitachi digger beside a large hole, near a pile of debris. You look into the hole—*and you cannot remember what used to be there!*

A slight panic sets in: Was there *ever* anything there? Or is this the true nature of the neighbourhood—a series of black holes, waiting to be revealed?

What an odd feeling. It is as though disappearance has become such a mainstay of our culture that our memories are fading away, we are disappearing ourselves.

Nobody wants to sound like Prince Charles on an anti-development sniff, but let us not pretend that these things have no effect. Beauty and harmony help you; ugliness hurts you. Culture is a powerful force that is never neutral. It can keep you sane, and it can drive you crazy.

This is not a hard concept for *other* countries to grasp.

A member of a 1970s rock group purchased a historic castle outside London, England, and proceeded to renovate it to his requirements, gutting the building and installing an indoor swimming pool, an exercise room, a recording studio and other improvements. The village had no objection to any of this—that is, until the owner tried to removed two stone dogs that stood by the entrance.

This simply would not do. The villagers had been looking at those dogs for generations; had passed them every day to and from work. The wealthy young man was welcome to alter the inside of the castle—it was his castle, he had bought and paid for it—but he was not free to alter the view, *because the view belongs to everybody.*

Imagine trying to sell that to a Canadian businessman.

We lack a social contract when it comes to the view—or to any other part of the cultural environment that forms the imaginary nation. There is no law to protect our sanity. Our inner lives can be made poorer, uglier and more boring by somebody else, at their convenience, *and there is nothing we can do about it.*

If we could choose what we see and hear and *assume* about life, things might be different, but we cannot. What can you do? When in Rome, or when Rome is on TV, do what the Romans do. All in all, it is not so bad. We can take it.

After all, it's free.

But there comes a point in any deteriorating cultural landscape when ordinary people, who have jobs and mow their lawns and pay taxes, notice their lives becoming more squalid with each passing year. It is a nasty feeling, and there is nothing to be done about it—as long as the cultural choices are defined someplace else, as long as these choices are limited to that which is acceptable to sponsors, developers and bureaucrats.

In Eastern Europe, this longing, this pang of aesthetic desire—for tastier food, better toilets, something nice to look at, clothes that fit—initiated a cultural revolution which has barely begun. (Now they are discovering the hidden price of that Walkman in the window.)

In Canada we are at the stage where we have become grumpy. Our sense of meaning has been squandered, the social contract has been shattered, clear-cuts continue both rural and urban, but we are not prepared to do anything yet, other than to vote *against* the incumbent regime. In between elections we hunker down in our powerlessness and try to ignore the hump, outwardly playing down the significance of the imaginary Canada we know to be there, in order to minimize our own stature, to duck our implied responsibility to the human race and to the earth.

But we are not happy about it. Like the dug-out lot with the Hitachi digger beside it, we stare into the empty hole that was our shared idea, and although the memory is hazy we know that something used to be there.

What was there, although we would never have been so pretentious as to give it such a lofty title, was the indigenous culture of a country.

Canadian culture differs from British culture in that it does not assume inequality as fundamental to stability, nor as a God-given right. On the other hand, we differ from American culture in that we make no claim that all men, let alone all persons, are born equal. You can be poor and it may not be your fault.

Instead, Canada developed on the foundation of what George Orwell once referred to as *common human decency.*

In Canada we traditionally believe that free competition must occur within the boundaries of common human decency. If a competing farmer and his family arrive at our door hungry, cold or sick, common human decency demands that we take them in. As a country we extend this courtesy to all our citizens—even when we suspect that our neighbours are not quite as hungry or as sick as they claim to be; even when we suspect that they may have a few chickens hidden in the barn.

Common human decency means living with the idea that someone else may be getting the better of the deal. It means saying "excuse me" when somebody bumps into *you* on the sidewalk. It means saying "I'm sorry" at times when there is really no reason to.

I am trying to describe a fundamental position of goodwill, a spaciousness that makes compromise and accommodation possible; it is the underlying basis for our extraordinary social stability, our relative non-violence, our comparative lack of dreadful poverty, our comparably liveable cities.

The Canadian government did not create these habitual virtues; Canadian people did.

Canadian culture will never make gripping action drama. If you want to undermine a good thriller, sympathize with the person getting shot. The audience wants to see the bad guy fall down dead; Canadians tend to point the camera at his or her grieving parents.

On the other hand—and I am shocked by this as much as anyone—entertainment may not be the most important thing in life. It may not even be the most important thing on television. It may be far more important that we communicate, reminding each other on a regular basis that, in the Canada we hold in our minds, the Canada we all want to live in, *it's OK to be nice.* In the long run, you will be further ahead. You are not necessarily being taken for a sucker, because this is the way we make things *work.*

I can hardly believe I just wrote that. It is so wimpy, so United Church, so *Canadian.* But tell that to the Somalians, the

Bosnians, the Georgians and Indonesians. The decade contains plenty of excitement and spectacle to stimulate the adrenalin and to stop the heart. With all that world-class entertainment on offer, how odd that so many citizens of other countries want to come to Canada. To hear them, you would think such a place exists.

How to Make Things Work

In Canada today we face a decision far greater than any election: Can we bring the two Canadas back together—the one we hold in our imagination and the one we grit our teeth over while reading the newspaper? Are we going to accept ourselves as a real country, or not?

With our educational and cultural institutions, our degree of socialization and our standard of living, Canada can lead the world in environmental quality, social justice, education and re-education—if we really want to. We can create the city of God.

That was the idea, was it not? The true north strong and free? New hope for the human race?

I wonder. It is so much easier to sit in the suburbs of the North American marketplace, complain about the deficit and watch TV. Leave the meaning of our lives to the entertainment industry, the tourists, let the market decide—anything rather than take responsibility for it ourselves.

Culture is like a leprechaun. If you fail to pay attention it gets away from you, blending with the current ideology, whether it is the heroic materialism of the right, the progressive puritanism of the left, or the monetarist mysticism of the marketplace. Canadian culture becomes a commodity, a drug, a propaganda tool or simply an issue of "personal choice." But sooner or later it dawns on even the most video-scrambled mind that it is far more than all those things put together.

Our culture is our mental freedom to *make* choices, the philosophical basis upon which we decide what is important and take responsibility for ourselves. Culture is what we mean, as social beings on earth.

Culture is not just a playground for artists and enthusiasts. It is the concern of every citizen because, whether we accept this or not, *we are all works of art.*

Like it or not, we create and recreate ourselves. We are responsible for the shape and meaning of our lives. Passive or active, decisive or indecisive, you and I are the authors of what we become, and the same criteria by which critics judge works of art apply to our lives as well.

Are we interesting or banal? Are we original, or a copy of someone else? Do the various forces that make up our lives work together, or are we rendered ineffective by internal conflicts? Do we have integrity, or do we tell people whatever they will pay to hear? Do we have something to say to the world, to give to other people, or are we just trying to make money?

And, in the end, what do our lives add up to? Do they make a good story? Are our lives memorable? Or should the world just count us out?

We are all works of art, cultural creations. We need to pay attention—to each other, to the world we are in the process of creating, to the culture that surrounds us and draws us imaginatively together, that can give us the spiritual strength to face a world of shifting borders and changing times.

After all, we are here together. This is how we will be remembered. The imaginary country will last a very long time. And life is short.

And—oh dear—I am afraid there will be reviews.

Epilogue

According to a recent report in *The Vancouver Sun,* the Standing Committee on Citizenship and Immigration—the architects of my humiliation via teleconference some months ago—has proposed that dual citizenship with other countries be outlawed by Ottawa, in the hope that this new attempt at eliminating the hyphen once and for all will finally imbue Canadians with an imperative sense of "national pride." The measure would force Canadians, arbitrarily, but for their own good of course, into an absolute identification with the parentland that has hitherto eluded them.

I nearly spilled my coffee.

Talk about adding insult to injury. So this was what those electronic, bilingual tête-a-têtes in rented boardrooms from coast to coast were leading to!

Talk about the "garrison mentality": For me, a so-called "Canadian nationalist," such a rat-in-a-trap version of citizenship causes the heart to die a little—the way it sinks when you encounter someone who agrees with you one hundred per cent, but whom you find personally repugnant.

The proposal to eliminate dual citizenship naturally produced immediate shrieks of alarm from the Bloc Québécois, who quickly saw the implications of such a change to the ongoing, delicately-hyphenated aspirations of Quebecers. Of course the Bloc conveniently chose to ignore the fact that the Parti Québécois plans to impose an identical choice on Quebecers—to terminate their capacity to ride the sovereignty-association hyphen in either direction, their freedom to choose connection or independence, *depending on the situation.*

And thanks to its chronic state of mild paranoia, the Bloc failed to recognize that their objections on behalf of Quebec applied just as legitimately to other Canadians, whose hyphenated status is as real and important to them as it is to Quebecers, and who likewise regard the Ottawa presence as a colonial hallucination at some distance from real life, as it is lived in real villages.

Ironically, for French- and English-Canadians alike, to eliminate the hyphen from their existence would be to erase once and for all the very thing that makes them peculiarly Canadian.

Thanks to Canada's vast array of geographical and historical circumstances, the imaginary country has evolved here in a way that is curiously un-European—almost Asian in its spiritual dimensions. To be a Canadian is to be free to change one's identity, *depending on the situation*; to see or not to see, *depending on the situation*; to act out our ancestral cultural roots or our "Canadian identity," *depending on the situation*; to live in a dream or in the real world, *depending on the situation*.

Americans view this comparative lack of a set national ego on our part as drab moderation—just as most North Americans mistakenly view Asian forms of social harmony in terms of regimentation and conformity. Canadians, overwhelmed as they are by American culture, have too often accepted this jaundiced foreign view of themselves; in fact it is highly Canadian of us to exclaim "How Canadian!" in a derogatory fashion, as though referring to somebody else.

Shamed by our lack of monolithic Canadian substance, we are intermittently tempted by would-be saviours to validate only one side of our hyphen, to seize upon only one fragment of our diffuse, ephemeral Canadian identity and to make do with that for life—when, ironically, *the hyphen itself* forms the essence of the Canadian style.

Canadians have always ultimately recoiled from such binary choices whenever they are offered, saying "no" in both official languages to the 1980 Quebec referendum and to the Charlottetown Accord alike. Had Trudeau's repatriation of the constitution been subjected to a similar vote, no doubt the thing would still be in Westminster—but he didn't bother to ask.

Sensing their peril, despite pressure from multinational economic forces, the ambitions of political and business leaders and the recommendations of all sorts of lofty panels and commissions, Canadians stubbornly cling to their dualism, their freedom to choose between their individual selves and their collective selves—*depending on the situation*.

Canadians even manage to resist the siren song of would-be pundits like myself, who would have them internalize and protect some imagined virtue as their exclusive cultural property. Indeed, were I to face the Standing Committee again (God forbid) with my nuggets of Canadiana, expressing the values of citizenship to prospective immigrants, my advice would be: Don't let *anyone* tell you what a Canadian is, including me.

192

You never know what the future will bring, what survival skills it might require. Better to keep an open mind, however vague the options might seem. Uniquely in Canada, two birds in the bush are worth one in the hand.

The mental challenge is to keep both birds out there in view, and to resist the urge to throttle one of them with your fist.

In my Quixotic assault on the Canadian identity, my attempt to persuade the reader that a truer Canada is located in the imagination—as opposed to the officially interconnected web of static institutions that constitutes the nation-state—I blundered into the Ottawa trap. I created a classic example of analogue-digital confusion, presenting the two sides of a theoretical debate and inviting the reader to choose my personal favourite, when the real choices to be made by Canadians are as diffuse and momentary as Canada itself. They move like beams of light among people and institutions coping with this immense geography, trying to keep in touch with a landscape that is itself alive and moving.

Our ancestors hated and feared this living landscape, and created institutions to protect themselves from its overwhelming power—a power that defies all mental imagery, all European terms of measurement. The first settlers could no more hold in their minds a true picture of the space that confronted them than a map of Canada can contain or convey the physical, living presence of the arctic tundra in its resonant silence, or the Fraser River, that great tawny serpent writhing its way to the sea.

Unwilling to trade ideas with the Earth People and to borrow their native spiritual vocabulary, our ancestors made the best of it with mechanical ingenuity and gritted teeth. They built the self-contained village with its back to the wild, its church spires challenging the surrounding trees, and its set of unspoken codes—social habits of sufficient strength to ensure that their descendants, generations later, would refuse to move out, even with no jobs in their village to support them.

Having made a secure bed for themselves at home, our forebears constructed a railroad to link their villages. Two hyphens of steel were hammered into the ground so that trains—moving villages—could clatter from coast to coast without seeming to go anyplace at all. Gentlemen in spats and cutaways could sleep in velvet Victorian coaches and eat on linen tablecloths from Toronto to Winnipeg, through muskeg that would have made a meal of them in a matter of hours.

Yet even then, something about the geography continued to fascinate them irresistibly. Despite houses, railways, highways and telephones, our ancestors could never bring themselves to declare complete victory over the landscape. Villagers regularly went on tenting and fishing excursions; churches established scout troops and summer camps; and CPR passengers stared eagerly out their windows for a glimpse of the wild.

Responding to its charisma, the Group of Seven painted wilderness landscapes, to the scorn of their European critics; Frederick Philip Grove wrote *Over Prairie Trails*, about negotiating the *space between* his Manitoba home and the school where he taught; and Pauline Johnson recited to large crowds all over the country, under the Native stage name, Tekahionwake.

Even today, when air travel protects us from even a single glimpse of the landscape between villages—a landscape that still comprises almost the entire country—professionals pay large sums of money to vacation in crude summer cottages, on northern Ontario lakes infested with blackflies. Vancouver computer operators on their lunch break jostle for a glimpse of an eagle flying over Burrard Inlet. University students in Canada receive degrees in geography, when such a major is rarely even offered in the United States.

The fact that we have garrisoned ourselves against the landscape does not mean that we have forgotten or lost it: On the contrary, it amounts to a profound, if grudging, acknowledgement of its vital power. We may not wish to travel north, but part of us can never forget that it is there, and when an American icebreaker crosses the Arctic we are as alarmed as if it were a destroyer invading the St. Lawrence Seaway. Even in metro Toronto, the landscape cannot be completely ignored, with snow to be shovelled and slush and wind to be negotiated with ungainly galoshes and infantile toques.

The landscape makes us clumsy. It always has. Nothing we wear feels entirely comfortable as we totter between fear and fascination.

Our two European official languages, driven by the verb *to be*, which creates and assumes a world of static, immutable things, fail utterly to capture the constant state of transformation that characterizes our physical country—its vital quality, the sense that we are surrounded by a living thing. Yet as any weekend camper knows, it is impossible to spend a single night in the forest without acknowledging its animate character, as human-sounding voices echo in the distance, faces appear in rocks and in the bark of trees, and the moon emits its silent, anguished *oh*.

And as we open our eyes, scratch our insect bites and stare up from our sleeping bags at the grey morning sky, nothing is quite the same as we thought it was the previous day; everything around us is in the process of coming or going, growing or rotting away.

With language as with the weather, we made the best of inadequate tools: We created a hyphenated national vocabulary, a verbal railway to allow the mind to move from one alternative to the next in constant motion, back and forth. With sovereignty-association as with nature, the hyphen allows Canadians, however awkwardly, to go forward, backward, or to writhe about someplace in between.

Yet the language continues to tug at us, to hold us back, for the European reader habitually reads from left to right, placing the hyphenated modifier *in front of* the thing modified, as in "Scottish-Canadian": The Scottish part seems preeminent, as though the person is Scottish and, by the way, also Canadian.

However, there are many situations, from voting to going to the hospital, in which the adjective "Canadian" comes first. This reverse reading of the hyphen is what enables Canadian peacekeeping forces overseas to perform as something other than an imperialist threat. The fact that they do not represent a monolithic culture, that most of us have at least some roots in foreign soil, gives our troops their reputation for fair dealing—to the point where an unjust killing in Somalia (surely a military commonplace, for we are dealing with heavily-armed young men) sends us into agonies of self-examination. By contrast, the US admitted no such humiliation when their navy destroyed an innocent passenger jet in the Middle East; nor does Britain blush at the Black and Tans' treatment of suspected IRA "terrorists." And try to explain Canada's handling of the affair to a South Korean.

Of course, as with the "Canadian identity," Canadians take the jaundiced viewpoint of an imagined outsider: We take no satisfaction in our armed forces' openness to criticism; nor do we take pride in their relatively high standard of behavior. Rather, we declare them to be either goons for allowing such a thing to happen, or incompetents for allowing us find out about it. *How Canadian!*

Similarly, when we express our capacity to see and not to see, we are tempted to regard the resulting mental image as one of hypocrisy; yet when we read the phrase in reverse—as "not to see *and also to see*"—we recognize the existence of a larger, unattainable dimension to things. "To not see *and also to see*" is to hope and to dream: the stuff of seers and poets, and not to be sniffed at.

The hyphen is our clumsy attempt to express something we know to be eternally mobile in the static declarative terms of the Iron People. As such it is pathetically inferior to the transformers and tricksters who animate the imagery of the Earth People. But a hyphen is better than nothing, for at least it affords us *some* motion.

Like our galoshes and toques, it is an ungainly Canadian fashion statement that nevertheless enables us to walk safely to the Town Pantry during a blizzard; unlike the fellow in the telegenic James Dean T-shirt, frozen stiff by the fire hydrant in Buffalo.

Our ungainly yet irresistible dance with the Canadian landscape continues today, even when the insulating process, initiated in the pioneer village, has reached new dimensions.

Thanks to electronics, satellite technology and fibre optics, the available devices for transcending our immanent geography have become more and more sophisticated. Now we have access to a modem world in which we all inhabit a state of virtual reality, with no distance between anyone and everyone, in which everyone from Chile to Chad drinks from and pours into the same information pool:

> I'd like to teach the world to sing
> In perfect harmony;
> I'd like to buy the world a Coke,
> And keep it company....

It is no accident that Canada aspired to world leadership in telecommunications technology, and that Ottawa is on its way to becoming Silicon Valley North. Nor is it an accident that a Canadian coined the term "the Global Village"—describing technology's triumphant denial of space and geography. From the moment the first European set foot on North America to name

196

parts of it after European cities and royals, Canadians have been into virtual reality in a big way. The Global Village is nothing more than Canadian culture writ large.

Marshall McLuhan displayed a highly Canadian ambivalence about the Global Village, whose sinister influence goes well beyond its homogenizing banality—the force that replaces a railway station in Truro with a strip mall. What makes the Global Village a potential threat to us all is the fact that life's most crucial realities *can never be rendered in virtual terms*. There is no virtual shelter against the cold; there is no virtual food, water or air. The human race cannot survive on virtual reality alone. Virtual reality is a *product*, like Coca-Cola and the Liberal Party of Canada. It can never be "the real thing."

What I am saying is that perhaps this is not the time for Canadians to take masochistic delight in their country's current turmoil. Maybe we have not blown it as badly as we think we have. We may have found ourselves at the leading edge of a very large human experiment, charting new territory as model citizens of the Global Village.

In that sense, the current crisis of Canada's political and social institutions, the disappearing act now being performed by the Canadian nation-state, may be seen as a birth, not a death: not as the shattering of a doomed social enterprise, but as the cracking of an egg.

After all, the hyphen goes both ways—between anxiety and hope, between dying and being born. That disgruntled rustling we hear all over the land may not be a death rattle; it may be the sound of the hidden people, emerging cautiously and clumsily from the warm confinement of their imaginary shell to face the world, to demonstrate what they have learned:

That the earth lives and moves—it is not a dead rock upon which to take a final stand. That living skillfully entails constant motion—negotiating as the situation demands. That it is neither necessary nor advantageous to have a fixed identity, to be pinned wriggling to the wall by a single declarative sentence containing the verb *to be*.

That the world is not a thing to be manipulated and used. It is bigger than us. Like Canada, it is a living, ancient land.